"We need ne... know," he s...

Wasn't this what she'd wanted to hear? Some talk of commitment? Of permanence? What else could he mean? They'd spent a wonderful night together and at least as far as she was concerned, it was much more than that.

"What, not even to eat or have a bath?" she asked lightly, while her heart pounded like a steam engine inside her.

"I'm being serious." He lay flat on his back with his hands folded behind his head. "We could get married," he said. "I mean it makes sense, don't you think? We're compatible in bed, more than compatible, and it could sort out every niggling area of all this bargaining over the business that we've been trying to do over the past few weeks. I can't personally think of a better arrangement than marriage."

*Getting down to business
in the boardroom...and the bedroom!*

A secret romance, a forbidden affair,
a thrilling attraction...

What happens when two people work together
and simply can't help falling in love—
no matter how hard they try to resist?

Find out in our new series of stories
set against working backgrounds.

This month in

Merger by Matrimony
by
Cathy Williams

Cathy Williams

MERGER BY MATRIMONY

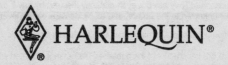
HARLEQUIN®

TORONTO • NEW YORK • LONDON
AMSTERDAM • PARIS • SYDNEY • HAMBURG
STOCKHOLM • ATHENS • TOKYO • MILAN • MADRID
PRAGUE • WARSAW • BUDAPEST • AUCKLAND

ISBN 0-373-12222-5

MERGER BY MATRIMONY

First North American Publication 2001.

This edition published by arrangement with Harlequin Books S.A.

® and TM are trademarks of the publisher. Trademarks indicated with
® are registered in the United States Patent and Trademark Office, the
Canadian Trade Marks Office and in other countries.

Visit us at www.eHarlequin.com

Printed in U.S.A.

CHAPTER ONE

THE grey-haired man was looking lost and bewildered. From her vantage point in the classroom, and looking over the heads of the fifteen pupils who had shown up for school, Destiny Felt could see him staring around him, then peering at the piece of paper in his hand, as if searching for inspiration which had been lost somewhere along the way. Rivulets of perspiration poured down his face, which was scrunched up in frowning, perplexed concentration, and his shirt bore two spreading damp patches under the arms.

He was ridiculously attired for the belting heat, she thought. Long trousers, a long-sleeved shirt which had been ineffectively rolled to the elbows. The only sensible thing about his clothing was the broad-brimmed hat which produced at least some shade for his face, even though he looked ridiculous in it.

What on earth was he doing in this part of the world? Visitors were virtually non-existent—unless they were photo-happy tourists, which this man didn't appear to be—and as far as she was aware they were not expecting any new medics or teachers to the compound.

She continued viewing his antics for a few minutes longer, watching as he shoved the paper into the briefcase which he'd temporarily stood on the scorching ground at his side before tentatively making his way to the first open door he saw.

Her father would not welcome the intrusion, she thought, continuing to eye the stranger as he knocked hesitantly on the door before pushing through. She fought down the temptation to abandon her class and hotfoot it to her father's research quarters, and instead she reverted her attention to the motley assortment of children.

All would be explained, and sooner rather than later. In a compound comprised of a mere fifteen working adults, nothing was a secret, least of all the appearance of a foreigner obviously on a mission of some sort.

The overhead fan, which appeared to be on the point of total collapse from old age, provided a certain amount of desultory, sulky relief from the heat, but she could still feel the humid air puffing its way through the open windows. No wonder the poor man had looked as though he'd been about to faint from heat exhaustion.

By the time she was ready to dismiss her class, she too was feeling in desperate need of a shower, not to mention a change of clothes.

In fact, she was heading in the direction of her quarters when she heard the clatter of footsteps along the wooden corridor of the school house.

'Destiny!' Her father's voice sounded urgent.

'Just coming!' Damn. She hoped she wasn't about to be palmed off with the hapless man. This was her father's famous ploy. To offload perfect strangers, when they showed up for whatever reason, on her, and whenever she complained about it he would cheerfully brush aside her objections with a casual wave of the hand and a gleeful remark along the lines of how blessed he was to have an obliging daughter such as her.

The three of them very nearly catapulted into one another round the bend in the corridor.

'Destiny...'

She glanced at the man, then turned her full attention

to her father, who favoured her with an anxious smile. 'Just about to go and have a shower, Dad.'

'Someone here to see you.'

Destiny slowly turned to face the man whose hand had shot out towards her. She was at least six inches taller than him. Not an unusual occurrence. She was nearly six feet, and in fact there were only four people on the compound taller than her, including her father, who looked positively towering next to the stranger.

'Derek Wilson. Pleased to meet you.'

'Don't you speak Spanish?' Destiny asked politely, in Spanish.

'Now, don't start that, darling.' Her father remonstrated with her absent-mindedly, and removed his spectacles to give them a quick clean with the corner of his faded, loose shirt.

'Well…people come here expecting us all to speak their tongue…'

'He's from England. Of course he's going to come here speaking English.' There was a lazy, affectionate familiarity to their debate, as though they'd been down this road a thousand times before but were nevertheless more than happy to tread along it once again, through sheer habit if nothing else. 'Apologies for this child of mine,' her father said in impeccable English. 'She can be very well behaved when she puts her mind to it.'

Derek Wilson was staring at her with a mixture of alarm and fascination. It was a reaction to which she'd grown accustomed over time. Nearly every outsider who set foot on the compound regarded her in the same manner, as if, however bowled over they were by her looks, they still suspected that she might target the next blow-dart in their direction.

'What do you want?'

'Social niceties, darling? Remember?'

'It's taken me for ever to track you down.'

The man glanced between the two of them, and her father obligingly capitulated, 'Perhaps we should discuss this somewhere more comfortable. Get some refreshment for you…you must be done in after your trek to get here.'

'That would be super.'

Destiny could feel his eyes on her as the three of them strode through the school house, attracting curious looks from the pupils in disarray as they gathered their scant books and bags together to go home. The noise was a babble of tribal Spanish, a beautiful, musical sound that seemed very appropriate to the beautiful, coffee-complexioned children with their straight black hair and expressive black eyes.

It was why she'd always stood out, of course. Not just her height, but her colouring. Fair-skinned, choppy sun-streaked fair hair, green eyes. And of course, in the depths of Panama, a white face was always a novelty.

'In case you hadn't guessed, this is our local school,' her father was saying, much to her astonishment. Playing the tour guide had never been one of his chosen pastimes. He'd always left that to her mother, whose death five years previously was still enough to make her feel choked up. 'We have a fairly static number of pupils. Of course, as you might expect, some are more reliable than others, and a great deal depends on the weather. You would be surprised how the weather can wreak havoc with day-to-day life over here.'

Derek Wilson's head was swivelling left to right in an attempt to absorb everything around him.

'Just to the right of the school house we have some medical facilities. All very basic, you understand, but we've always lacked the finance to really do what should be done.'

This was her father's pet topic. Money, or rather the lack of it, to fund the medical facilities. He was a researcher and a gifted doctor and had a complete blind eye to anyone who couldn't see that money should be no object when it came to questions of health.

They'd reached the little outer room that served as an office for her father, and he settled the man in a chair then bustled to the stunted and rusting fridge in the corner of the room so that he could extract a jug of juice. A small breeze fluttered through the two large, open windows which were opposite one another so as to maximise air draft, and Derek Wilson attempted to ventilate himself by flapping his shirt at the collar.

Poor man, Destiny thought with a twinge of sympathy. For whatever reason, he'd probably left behind a family in England and all mod cons so that he could tramp halfway across the world to Panama, still a mysterious and unfathomable land virtually behind God's back, and deliver a message to her.

What message?

She felt a little stirring of unease.

Her father handed her a glass of highly sweetened fruit juice, and she attempted to catch his eye for a non-verbal explanation of what was going on, but he was in a strange mood. Nervous, she thought, but trying hard not to show it.

Why?

Another flutter of apprehension trickled along her spine, defying her attempts to laugh it off.

'Well.' Derek cleared his throat and looked in her direction. 'Very nice place you have here...'

'We think so.' She narrowed her eyes on him.

'Brave of you to live here, if you don't mind me saying...'

She shot a look at her father, who was staring abstractedly through the window and providing absolutely no help whatsoever.

'Nothing brave about it, Mr Wilson. Panama is one of the most beautiful countries in the world. Every day there's something new and wonderful to see and the people are very gentle and charming. So you needn't be scared of being captured and tortured or chopped up into little loin steaks and eaten.'

'I never imagined that for a moment...' he protested, and this time when he looked at her his eyes were shrewd and speculative.

'What did you come here for?' she asked bluntly, at which her father tore his attention away from the scenery of grass and dirt and beyond the compound the dense forest that housed the people who seemed as familiar to them as the Westerners who lived and worked alongside them in the compound.

'I've brought something for you.' He rifled through his briefcase and extracted a thick wedge of cream, heavy-duty paper, covered with small type, which he handed to her. 'Have you ever heard of Abraham Felt?'

'Felt...Abraham? Yes, vaguely... Dad...?' she said slowly, scanning the papers without really seeing anything.

'Abraham Felt was my brother, your uncle,' her father interjected tightly. He took a few deep breaths. 'Well, perhaps I'd better let the professional do the explaining.'

'What explaining?'

'Abraham Felt died six months ago. He left a will. You are the main beneficiary.'

'Oh. Is that all? Couldn't you have put it in writing?

Post might take a while to get here, but it arrives eventually.'

'No, Miss Felt, you don't understand.' He gave a small laugh which he extinguished by clearing his throat. 'His estate is worth millions.'

The silence that followed this statement was broken only by the sound of birds and parrots cawing, the muffled voices of people criss-crossing the compound, and the distant rush of the river which provided the only form of transport into the heart of the forest.

'You're joking.' She smiled hesitantly at her father, who returned her smile with off-putting gravity. 'Aren't you?'

'I'm a lawyer, Miss Felt. My line of business doesn't include jokes.'

'But what am I supposed to do with all that money?' Her laugh was a bit on the hysterical side. 'Look around you, Mr Wilson. Do you see anything to spend money on here? We all get a government grant, and some of the locals make things for the tourist trade, but as for spending millions…no shops, no fast cars, no restaurants, no hotels…no need.'

'It's not quite as easy as that.' He rested his elbows on his knees and contemplated her thoughtfully. He'd removed a handkerchief from his pocket and proceeded to give his face a thorough wipe with it. She could see the beginnings of sunburn. In this heat, sunblock was only partially successful. She'd always used it but, even so, at the age of twenty-six, she was as brown as a nut— a smooth, even brown that the average sun-seeker would have killed for.

'Aside from a multitude of small interests, his country estate and a collection of art work, there's his major holding. Felt Pharmaceuticals. It has offshoots in some six

European countries and employs thousands of people. I have the precise figures here if you want. And it's in trouble. Big trouble. Now there's a takeover in the offing, and who's to say how many jobs will be lost globally? As the main beneficiary, nothing can be done without you.'

'I don't know a thing about business,' she said stubbornly, willing her father to chip in with some much needed support.

'Your father says that you were a child prodigy.'

Destiny shifted uncomfortably in her chair and sat on her hands. 'Dad! How could you?'

'You were, my darling, and you know it. Even that boarding school didn't know what to do with you…and perhaps the time has come for you to spread your wings a bit. It's all well and good working out here and…'

'No!'

'Listen to me, Destiny!' Her father's voice cracked like a whip and startled her. She stared at him open-mouthed. 'At least go to England and see what this is all about. You'll have to go there anyway to claim this inheritance…'

'But I don't want any inheritance! I don't want to go *anywhere!*'

The heat in the room began to feel suffocating and she stood up, agitated, lifting her face to the fan so that it whirled her hair back and soothed her hot skin. Her baggy dress seemed to cling to her even though she knew it wasn't. Under it, she could feel perspiration trickle from beneath the heavy folds of her breasts down to the waistband of her sensible cotton underwear.

'If you hate it, you can always come back here,' her father was telling her in a gentler voice, 'but don't turn your back on an experience just because you're afraid.

We've always taught you to see the unknown as a challenge and not as a threat.'

'And besides,' Derek chipped in slyly, 'think of the benefits to your father's research, should you have your hand on the steering wheel of an important pharmaceutical company. Your father has told me that he's working on a cure for certain tropical diseases using special tree saps and plant derivatives. Funding would cease to be a problem. You could help these indigenous tribes far more than you ever could by staying put.' He crossed his legs and began to fan himself with his hat, exposing a balding head that was at odds with his reasonably unlined face. 'Come to England, Miss Felt, for your father if nothing else...'

And that had been the carrot, as the wretched man had known it would be.

Even so, one week later, and sitting bolt upright on an aeroplane which had taken her two days of long-distance hiking to get to, she still couldn't fathom out whether she was doing the right thing or not.

She looked around her furtively and surprised a young tourist staring at her, at which she assumed an expression of worldly-wise disdain.

Ha! If he only knew. She and any form of worldly-wise experience had never so much as rubbed shoulders. Her life had always been a peripatetic journey on the fringes of civilisation, swept along by parents whose concerns had never included the things most normal people took for granted. Occasionally, when one of the members of their team took a trip into Panama City, they would return with a few magazines. She knew about microwave machines and high-tech compact disc players, but only from the glossy pages of the magazines. Firsthand, her experience of twenty-first-century living was lamentably undeveloped.

From Panama City they'd moved gradually onwards and downwards, to more and more remote towns, until they'd finally taken root amidst the wilderness of the Darien forest some eight years previously. In between her education had been erratic and mostly home-grown, aside from one tortuous year at a boarding school in Mexico and then a further three at the Panamanian university, from which she'd emerged, in record time, a qualified doctor and desperate to return to her family and the jungle she had come to love.

She'd hated the veneer of sophistication that seemed an obligatory part of twentieth-century city life. She'd hated the need to wear make-up and dress in a certain way at the risk of being thought freakish. She'd hated the envy she'd encountered from other girls who'd thought her too good-looking and too stand-offish for her own good, and the barely developed young men with their boorish, laddish manners who'd seemed hell-bent on getting her into bed. She'd had no real interest in shopping for clothes whenever she could, and neither school nor university had been able to cope with her prodigious talent at nearly everything she put her hands to.

So what was she going to now?

More of the same, and this time with the horrendous task of walking into a company about which she knew nothing, to attempt to speak to people about whom she knew nothing and all because of an inheritance from an uncle whom she had not known from Adam.

As she stepped off the plane and allowed the unfamiliarity of Heathrow Airport to wash over her like a cold shroud, she felt a wave of terror assault her.

Even her two disreputable cases rolling past on the belt

looked small and scared next to the bigger, brasher items of luggage being snatched up by the horde of weary travellers.

She was to stay at her unknown and now deceased uncle's Knightsbridge house which, Derek Wilson had assured her, was beyond plush.

Right now, all Destiny wanted was to be back home where she belonged.

She had to force her feet forwards, out through the line of watchful uniformed custom officers, past the heaving banks of friends and relatives waiting for their loved ones back from holiday and then, with a surge of gratitude, towards the familiar face of the man who had succeeded in turning her uncomplicated life on its head.

'Got here safe and sound, then,' Derek greeted her, assuming control of the trolley with her bags even though she was more than capable of pushing it herself. 'Did you have a chance to read all the company reports I left with you? Details of your inheritance? My driver's waiting for us outside. You'll probably want to relax after your trip—' he grimaced at the memory of his own '—so I thought I'd drop you straight to your house, let you sort yourself out, have a rest. I've made sure that it's fully stocked with food and you can give me a ring in the morning so that we can start sorting out this business.'

'Where are all these people *going*?' There was barely room to manoeuvre their trolley. In her brightly woven dress, which had been her only item of clothing suitable for long-distance travel, Destiny felt gauche, out of place and utterly lost.

'All over the world.' The man at her side cast a critical look at his companion. 'You'll have to do some shopping, you know. Especially for when you go into the offices…'

'Why? What's wrong with what I've got on?'

'Nothing! It's very charming, I'm sure. Just…not quite suitable…'

'Suitable for what?'

They had now cleared the interminable confines of the airport terminal, but outside things were no less frantic. Destiny felt as though she'd been catapulted onto another planet, where everything operated on the fast-forward button. Black cabs rushed past them; buses were pulling up and pulling away; cars were spilling out their contents of travellers and cases. She allowed herself to be led to a long sleek car quietly purring at the end of the drop-off kerb. It was a far cry from the communal four-wheel-drive Jeep she'd become accustomed to, with its unreliable windows, cracked plastic seats and coughing engine noises.

'Suitable for what?' she resumed, as soon as they were in the back of the car.

Derek coughed apologetically. 'Suitable for the board meeting you'll be attending tomorrow afternoon.'

'Board meeting? *Me? Attending?*' She spoke four languages, had taught any number of subjects over the years, and knew more about medicine and how to deliver it than most doctors, yet the thought of a board meeting was enough to send her into a panic attack. She was only twenty-six! She shouldn't *be* here!

'Well, perhaps *board meeting* is a bit of an over-statement…the directors just want to meet you, actually…'

'Can't *you* go? Or perhaps tell them that I'm ill? Jet lag…?' She could feel her heart lurching about inside her and had to take deep breaths. Inoculation, delivering babies, tending to the ill seemed a faraway excursion to Paradise.

Derek swept past her objections with practised ease. 'Their futures are at stake. Naturally they want to meet the person now in charge of the show...' He cleared his throat and she looked at him, aware that some other piece of not quite so innocuous information was about to come.

'There's also one other person I feel I ought to mention...'

'What other person...?'

'I'm sure you'll be able to handle him...' His voice failed to live up to any corresponding conviction.

'*Handle him?* Is he violent?'

At which Derek allowed himself to chuckle. 'Not violent, my dear girl. Not in the sense you think. His name's Callum Ross...his name crops up in the Company Report I left for you...'

'Sorry, I fell asleep on the plane.'

'He's...how to describe him?...he's a household name over here in the world of high finance and business. Quite a legend, in fact. He's managed to accumulate quite a number of companies in a remarkably short space of time...' He sighed and nervously patted his receding hair. 'The man's quite formidable, Destiny. Some have even described him as ruthless.' His expression conveyed the impression that he included himself in this number. 'When he wants something, he's reputed to go after it, no holds barred.'

'I've met types like that,' Destiny said slowly.

'Have you? Really?'

'Yes. They live in the jungle and they're called cougars. They don't hesitate to go for the kill.'

Derek didn't smile as she might have expected. Instead he nodded and said musingly, 'It's a more fitting descrip-

tion than you might think... At any rate, Callum Ross
has wanted your uncle's company for some time now, if
gossip in the City is to be believed, and he was very
nearly there. Papers had been drawn up, waiting for the
signature of your uncle—who had the poor timing to die
before he could validate anything. He's engaged to—
well...you could say your stepcousin...'

'*I have a cousin?*' She felt a sudden flare of excitement
at the thought of that.

'No. Not quite. Your uncle was married four times.
Stephanie White was the daughter of his most recent ex-
wife by her previous marriage. Stephanie's surname became Felt at the time when her mother married your uncle. At any rate, she has some shares in the company,
along with the directors, but the majority of the shares
are now under your control. What I'm saying, Destiny,
is that Callum Ross badly wants what is essentially *your*
company now. He's seen his opportunity slip away from
him through a blow of chance and he's going to be a
very disappointed man. Disappointed enough to be a
thorn in your side.'

'I don't understand *any of this.*' She hadn't been following the progress of the car, but she was now aware
that they were pulling up outside a gated crescent. A
guard approached them, nodded at something Derek held
out for him to see, and the impressive black wrought-iron
gates smoothly glided open, like a pair of arms stretching
out to reveal a tantalising secret. '*All these people!* I
just...'

'Want to go home...?'

She nodded mutely at him, dully taking in what she
knew, without really having to be told, was an expensive
clutch of houses. They curled in a semi-circular forma-
tion around a small, impeccably manicured patch of

green. All white, all three storeys tall, all sporting black doors and tidy front gardens sectioned off with more black wrought-iron gates. A few cars were parked here and there and they were all of the same ilk as the one she was currently in. Sleek, long and shiny. She felt a little ill at the sight of all the structured precision.

'You can't. At least not quite yet. Not until the business with the company is sorted out once and for all.'

'Why don't I just sell to this Callum man? Wouldn't that be the easiest thing to do?' She tore her miserable eyes away from her prospective neighbourhood and looked at Derek.

'If you do, there's a good chance he'll split the company up to maximise his profits if he decides to sell. The other thing is this—there's almost no way that he's going to invest in the work your father's doing.'

'But wouldn't *I* be able to fund it all myself? With whatever I make from the company?'

'After all debts have been cleared? Without the back-up of the facilities over here in the Felt labs? Unlikely. Anyway—' he assumed a tone of bonhomie '—enough of all that. You'll be meeting the man himself soon enough. Here's your place! Number twelve. Lucky twelve. In case you haven't noticed, there's no number thirteen. Superstition. Guess there's a lot of that from where you come? Folklore, superstition, etc?' He pushed open his door as soon as the car had stopped, then skipped around to open hers before bounding merrily up three steps to black door number twelve.

'Meeting the man soon enough?' Destiny repeated, as he opened the front door and stepped back to let her pass. 'When?' The driver had followed them with her cases which, on the highly polished black and white flagged entrance hall, looked even sadder and more forlorn than they had on the conveyor belt at the airport.

'Shall I do the guided tour?'

'When am I going to be meeting this man, Derek?'

'Ah, yes. Tomorrow, actually.'

'You mean with all the other...directors?'

'Not quite. Tomorrow morning. After you've seen me, as a matter of fact. Thought it might be best to size up the enemy, so to speak, before you meet the rest...'

The enemy. The enemy, the enemy, the enemy.

She hoped that Derek Wilson had been exaggerating when he'd said that, but somehow, she doubted it. Whoever Callum Ross was, he was obviously good at instilling fear. It was a talent for which she had no respect. In the compound, she'd become accustomed to working alongside everyone else to achieve the maximum. How could they ever hope to help anyone else if they were too busy playing power games with one another? Only the big cats in the jungle inspired fear, and that was all part of nature's glorious cycle.

For a man to stride around thinking that he could command other people into obedience was anathema to her.

By the time she'd explored the house, unpacked and investigated the contents of the superbly stocked fridge and larder, she had managed to distil some of her apprehension at what lay ahead.

If her father could see her now, she thought, he would probably faint. Before she left to return to Panama, she would make sure that he *did* see her. In these grand surroundings. It would give them something to chuckle about on those sultry, whispering evenings, with the sounds of wildlife all around.

And if Henri could see her, sitting at the kitchen table, with a delicate china cup of coffee in front of her—proper milk! Proper coffee! She smiled. Dear Henri, her soul-mate, just a handful of years older than her, who still flirted with her and jokingly proposed marriage every so often.

Her mind was still sabotaging all her attempts to concentrate on what had to be done before travelling back to Panama, when there was a sharp buzz of the doorbell.

It took a few seconds for her to realise that the buzz corresponded to someone at *her* door, then several seconds more to find herself at the door. Derek, who obviously now saw himself as her surrogate father, had warned her of sharks in the big city which were more lethal than the fishy variety, but she pulled open the door anyway.

It was an impulse which she instantly regretted.

The man standing in front of her, angled in shadows, was taller than she was. Tall and powerful with a sharply contoured, unsmiling face. He was wearing a lightweight suit in a dark colour, appropriate for the mild summer weather, but even his suit did little to conceal the aggressive, muscular lines of his body. She felt her pulses begin to race.

She should have looked through the peephole in the door, a small device pointed out to her through which she could determine whether any unexpected visitors were welcome or not. Despite security, not all visitors were welcome, Derek had told her. Naturally she'd forgotten all about the wretched thing.

'Yes?' She placed her body squarely in the entrance so that the man couldn't brush past her, although, judging from his size, he would have had little difficulty in doing just that if he wanted to.

For a few disconcerting seconds, the man didn't say a word. He just looked at her very thoroughly, lounging indolently against the doorframe, one hand tucked into his trouser pocket.

'Who are you and what do you want?' Destiny said tensely. 'The security guard is within shouting distance so don't even think of getting up to anything.'

'What sort of thing do you imagine I might be getting up to?' he asked coolly. 'A bit of forcible entry, perhaps? Some looting and pillaging?' His voice was deep and smooth.

'Goodbye.' She stepped back and began closing the door to find his hand placed squarely on it. An immovable force.

'Are you Destiny Felt?'

The question froze her, allowing him the opportunity to push the door back and step into the hall, where the overhead light revealed an even more intimidating face than she'd gleaned from the semi-obscure darkness outside. His features were perfectly chiselled and his eyes were a unique shade of blue, midnight-blue. Cold blue eyes fanned by thick black lashes. Lashes that matched the colour of his hair and which, combined with the sensual lines of his mouth, lent him a powerfully masculine attraction. She took a step backwards and glared belligerently at the man standing in front of her.

'What business is it of yours?'

'Destiny Felt, fresh from the Panamanian wilderness? Heir to an unexpected fortune? My, my, my. Lady Luck certainly chose to shine forth on you, didn't she?' He looked around him. 'So this is good old Abe's place. Quite the change for you, wouldn't you say?'

'If you don't tell me who you are, this instant, I'm calling the police.' She folded her arms, unconsciously defensive, and stared at the man. When he returned his wandering gaze to her, it was to inspect her with a thoroughness that bordered on intrusive. It didn't help matters that he was formally dressed while she was in a way too short faded shift, one of the few items of clothing she possessed. Her long legs were too exposed for comfort and, without the reassuring barrier of a bra, her heavy breasts pushed against the dress.

He narrowed his eyes thoughtfully. 'Can't you guess? Surely Wilson must have mentioned my name in passing?'

'You're Callum Ross, aren't you?' she said with dawning comprehension. 'You're Callum Ross, who arrogantly assumes that he can push his way into this house and take control. Am I right?' Her hands shifted from chest to hips and she outstared him with an expression of hostility that matched his own. 'The great and powerful Callum Ross who thinks…what? That he can troop in here uninvited and scare me senseless into doing whatever it is you want? Is that it? Terrify the poor half-witted Destiny Felt because she's all the way from the middle of nowhere and probably doesn't know how to use a knife and fork properly, never mind argue back with the formidable Mr Ross and his reputation for scaring his adversaries senseless?'

'Not quite,' he snarled, but he had flushed darkly in response to her hurled accusations.

'Well, it won't work, Mr Ross. I'm not intimidated by you and I don't intend to be scared into selling you the company if I don't choose to sell. Now, get out of this house before I call someone to throw you out.'

Instead of leaving, though, he moved towards her, and she fought to stand her ground. 'Very fiery,' he murmured, in a change of tone that was much, much more destabilising. He lifted one hand and casually toyed with a few strands of hair, rendering her even more immobile than she had been. 'My mother always told me never to play with fire,' he breathed silkily, 'but I feel on this occasion I might be forced to disregard her advice.' He laughed under his breath. 'Till we meet tomorrow...'

CHAPTER TWO

'AH, MISS FELT. So we meet again. In the light of day.'

Destiny had spent the previous two and a half hours in Derek Wilson's office, prey to stomach-cramping nerves at the prospect of seeing Callum Ross again, whilst trying to grapple with the complexities of her inheritance. His entrance had been preceded by only the most perfunctory of knocks, and now there he was, looming in the doorway like a dark predator in search of some easy prey. *Her,* in other words.

Derek had half-risen from his seat. 'Mr Ross. Good of you to come.' He looked at both their faces in consternation. 'What do you mean by *we meet again?* Do you two know each other?'

'Mr Ross saw fit to pay me an unexpected visit last night,' Destiny said tightly.

'That, Mr Ross, was quite unorthodox, as you must well know. I have all the relevant papers here and I object to you using intimidation to try and manipulate my client. This matter needs to be discussed in a rational, civilised—'

'Intimidation?' The dark eyebrows rose expressively as he said this and he made his way to the chair next to Destiny, settling into it without bothering to wait for an invitation to take a seat. 'Whatever makes you think that I would resort to intimidation to get what I want, Derek?'

She could feel his presence next to her like a strong, electrical current, hot and lethal, radiating out towards her.

'I didn't *intimidate* you, Miss Felt, did I?'

'Actually, it would take more than you to intimidate me, Mr Ross.' She reluctantly glanced sideways to him and met his eyes with as flat an expression as she could muster.

'Callum. Please. If we're to do business together, we might as well be on a first-name basis. Destiny...' The insolence was there again, softly underlining his slow, velvety pronunciation of her name. She'd dealt with all manner of danger in her life. Real danger. Danger from animals on the many occasions when she'd accompanied her father along the dark river in their *piragua,* to get deep into the heart of the forest to tend to someone. Danger from illnesses with the power to kill. She would not allow him to get under her skin now.

'It has not yet been established that you will be doing business with my client, Mr Ross. Whilst I appreciate that your plans to take over Felt Pharmaceuticals were dashed by Abe's untimely—'

'Perhaps I could have some privacy with...Destiny, Derek?' He tore his eyes away from the tall, striking blonde incongruously dressed in her multicoloured frock—if it could be called a frock—and briefly focused them on the man ineffectively glaring in his direction.

From the minute he'd heard about the existence of a woman who had landed her unexpected prize catch, the catch that he had worked ruthlessly to secure for himself only to see his efforts reduced to rubble, he'd been looking forward to meeting her. Looking forward to a seam-free, ludicrously easy deal. He'd had no doubts that a woman plucked from the wilds of a Panamanian forest would readily agree to the terms and conditions meticulously drawn up for the sale of the company. He had been curious, but not unduly worried by the temporary hitch in his plans.

Having met her the evening before, he was really still not unduly worried, but his curiosity, he'd discovered, now exceeded his original expectations.

Despite his resolve to talk business in as restrained a manner possible, he found that he was itching to be rid of Derek and his patter. Destiny Felt had unexpectedly stirred something inside his jaded soul and he wanted her to himself. Alone.

'I don't think that that's a very good idea, Mr Ross.' Valiant words, Destiny thought, but Derek was looking very twitchy. 'My client needs protecting...'

'Do you need protecting?' Once more the blue eyes enveloped her.

'I think what Derek means is that I've only skimmed the surface of the proposal you had in effect with my uncle. He doesn't want to see me taken advantage of.'

'I should think not!' Derek sounded horrified.

'Oh, nothing could be further from my mind.' His low laugh was not reassuring. In fact, it just upped the tempo of her already skittering pulses. 'So now we all understand each other. I'm not about to take advantage of your client, Derek, so you can leave us alone for a while to discuss matters in privacy.' There was a hard edge to his voice now, although his body was still relaxed and his smile didn't falter.

'It's all right, Derek,' she said, releasing him from his state of nervous tension before he exploded all over his pristine mahogany desk. 'I can take care of myself. If I need you, I can always give you a shout.'

'This is all highly unorthodox,' he faltered, fumbling with his tie and frowning disgruntledly but standing up anyway.

Callum shot him a soothing look from under his dark lashes. At least Destiny, watching him covertly, suspected that it was meant to be soothing. In reality, it just seemed to make Derek even more jittery. Or maybe that was the intention. She'd never had any opportunity to see first-hand how power, real power, worked. She was learning fast.

Her body was rigid with tension as the door closed behind her buffer and Callum slowly positioned his chair so that he was completely facing her now.

She looked at him steadily. For the second time in as few days, she felt utterly disadvantaged in what she was wearing. It had never really occurred to her that the highly coloured clothes she'd brought over with her would make her stand out like a sore thumb in a country where everyone—certainly everyone in the Wilson legal firm—seemed to be attired in shades of black, brown or navy blue. No wonder the man thought that she was a push-over.

'What's Derek told you about me?' he drawled, linking his fingers together on his lap and stretching out his long legs in front of him, so that they were very nearly touching hers, which she had tucked protectively under her chair.

'That you were on the verge of consolidating a bid for my uncle's company. That it all fell apart when he died.'

'That all?' He cocked his head to one side, as though listening for something she couldn't hear.

'What more is there?' she asked politely.

'No character assassination?'

'I'm not in the habit of repeating other people's personal opinions,' she said calmly.

'No, I can understand that. It would be a disaster in a compound of only a handful of people.'

'How do you know...?'

'I made it my business to find out before you came over here. Forearmed is forewarned, as the saying goes.' Actually, he had done nothing of the sort. His mention of a compound had been an inspired guess and he wasn't quite sure what he'd been hoping to achieve with his distortion of the truth. He suspected, darkly, that it was a desire to provoke some sort of reaction from her. He was accustomed to people responding to him, focusing on every word he had to say. He could feel niggling irritation now at his staggering lack of success in that department. She looked back at him with those amazing sea-green, utterly unreadable eyes.

'I hadn't expected you to have such a good grasp of English,' he said bluntly, veering away from the topic, watching as she tucked some hair behind her ears.

Destiny hesitated, uncertain at the abrupt ceasefire. 'My parents certainly always spoke to me in English, wherever we happened to be. They always thought that it was important for me to have a good grasp of my mother tongue. Of course, I speak Spanish fluently as well. And French, although my German's a bit rusty.'

'Isn't that always the case?' he said drily, and she glanced at him, surprised at his sudden injection of humour. With a jolt of discomfort, she realised that, although he had not chosen to display it, there was humour lurking behind the sensual lines of his mouth and she hurriedly averted her eyes.

'There are a number of French workers on the compound, but our German colleagues have been more sporadic so I haven't had the same opportunity to practise what I've learnt.'

'You've studied?'

That brought her back to her senses. Just when an unwelcome nudge of confusion was beginning to slip in. Did the man think that she was thick? Just because her lifestyle had been so extraordinary?

'From the age of two,' she said coolly. 'My parents were obsessive about making sure that my education didn't suffer because of the lifestyle they had chosen. Sorry to disappoint you. Now, getting back to business, I'm not qualified to agree to anything with you. I still have to see the company, meet the directors...'

'Do you know why Felt Pharmaceuticals has been losing money over the past five years?' he cut in, and when she shook her head he carried on, with no attempt to spare her the details. 'Shocking mismanagement. Cavalier and ill-thought-out overinvestment in outside interests with profits that should have been ploughed back into the company, interests that have all taken a beating...'

'How do you know that?'

'I made it my business to know.'

'Just like you made it your business to find out about me before I came over here?'

He didn't like being reminded of that little white lie and he uncomfortably shifted in his chair. 'Unless you've taken a degree course in business management, you might not be aware that taking over a company requires just a touch of inside knowledge on the company you're planning to take over.'

'That's common sense, not business management know-how,' Destiny informed him, riled by the impression she got that he was patronising her.

He swept aside her input. 'For the past five years old Abe, miserable bastard that he was, was bedridden and had more or less been forced to hand over control to his directors—who are good enough men when being told

what to do, but on their own wouldn't be able to get hold
of a pint of beer in a brewery.'

'What was the matter with him?'

'What was the matter with *whom?*' One minute mouth-
ing off at him with cutting efficiency, the next minute
looking like a vulnerable child. What the hell was this
woman all about? He had known enough women in his
lifetime not to be disconcerted by anything they said, did
or thought, for that matter, but Destiny Felt was suc-
ceeding in throwing him off balance. How could someone be forthright and secretive at the same time? He
nearly grunted in frustration. 'He had a stroke and never
really recovered,' Callum said. 'Of course, he remained
the figurehead for the company but his finger was no
longer on the button, so to speak.'

'At which point you decided to break into the scene,
once you'd checked out where the weak spots were,' she
filled in, reading the situation with the same logical clarity of thought that she'd inherited from both her parents.

'It's called doing business.'

'Business without a heart.'

'The two, I might as well warn you, in case you're
foolhardy enough to stick around, don't go hand in hand.'
He hadn't felt so alive in the company of a woman for
as long as he could remember. He sincerely hoped that
she stuck around, just long enough for him to enjoy the
peculiar sparring they were currently establishing that
was so invigorating, but not long enough to thwart his
plans. His eyes drifted from her face to the swell of her
breasts jutting out against the thin dress and he drew his
breath in sharply.

Dammit, he was engaged! He shouldn't be looking at
another woman's breasts, far less registering their fullness, mentally stripping her of her bra. The thought felt

almost like a betrayal and he glared at her with unvoiced accusation that she had somehow managed to lead his mind astray.

'Why did you call him a *miserable bastard?*'

'You won't be able to revive the company, you know,' he said conversationally, standing up and prowling through the office, casually inspecting the array of legal books carefully arranged in shelves along one wall, then moving behind the desk to the picture window and idly gazing through it. 'You haven't the experience or the funds. My offer is wildly generous, as Abe would have been the first to admit.' He turned around to look at her, perching against the window ledge. 'Wait much longer and you'll end up having to sell anyway, for a song, so it's in your interests to give it up sooner rather than later. And then you can get back to your jungle, where you belong. It's a different kind of jungle here. One I don't imagine you'll have a taste for.'

'This is more than just business profit for you, isn't it?' Destiny said slowly. 'You speak as if you hated my uncle. Did you? Why? What was he like?'

'Use your imagination. What sort of man wills his fortune to someone he's never met?'

'I was told that it was because I was his only blood relation. I gather he had no children of his own. He and my father weren't close, but I was his niece.' It had been a straightforward enough explanation from Derek, but Callum's words had given her pause for thought. Abraham Felt, after all, had never met her. He and her father had maintained the most rudimentary of contact over the years. Surely in all that time he should have filled his life with people closer and dearer, to whom his huge legacy would have been more fitting?

'He left it all to you because Abraham Felt was incapable of sustaining friendships.'

'He had hundreds of wives, for goodness's sake!'

'Four, to be exact.'

'Well, four, then. He must have shared *something* with them.'

'Beds and the occasional conversation, I should imagine. Nothing too tricky, though. He was noted for his contempt for the opposite sex.'

'How do you know that? No, don't tell me, you made it your business to find out. I'm surprised you have time to do any work, Mr Ross, since you seem to spend most of it ferreting out information on my uncle and his company.'

For a split second, Callum found himself verbally stumped by her sarcasm. Oh, yes. He had to confess that he was enjoying himself. How on earth the depths of a Panamanian forest had managed to satisfy this woman, he had no idea. She was sharp. He wondered what life on this compound of hers really was like. Having spent his entire life in concrete jungles, he wondered whether a close community in the middle of nowhere might not be a hotbed of conversations stretching into the wee hours of the morning. Not to mention sizzling sex. After all, what else was there to do? For years and years on end? Cut off from civilisation and surrounded by hostile nature?

'Actually, your dear uncle was always very vocal on most things, including his short-lived romances.'

'He left some shares to Stephanie Felt, your fiancée,' Destiny pointed out. 'What about the rest of his step-children?'

'There were none.'

She could feel unanswered questions flying around in

her head like a swarm of bees. There was something more personal to his desire to gain control of her company. What? And was her stepcousin all part of his plan? A useful arrangement because she brought shares with her? Not enough to enable him to gain downright control of the company if he married her, but enough to ensure that he remained active in whatever was happening within it. Active and, through Stephanie, with a voice.

Or was her bond to the company simply a coincidence? Was he in love with her?

She realised that intrigue was something she had so rarely encountered it was a job grappling with it all now.

'What is Stephanie like?' she asked guilelessly.

'You'll meet her soon enough. This afternoon, in fact. With the rest of the fools.'

What kind of a non-answer was that? she wondered.

The door was pushed open and Derek's face popped around it. 'Had enough time, Mr Ross?' He didn't wait for an answer. Instead, he walked in and quietly shut the door behind him.

Not nearly enough, Callum felt like saying, but in fact he was already running late. Stephanie would be at the restaurant in under fifteen minutes. He felt an irrational surge of irritation rise to his throat, but he swallowed it and smiled politely at Derek.

'We'll need to continue this conversation after you've met your people,' he addressed Destiny, pushing himself away from the window and almost throwing the little Derek into shadow as he strolled past him towards the door. 'My offer still stands, but, like I said, don't leave it too late or you might find that I'm forced to reduce it.'

At which he saluted them both and left, not bothering to shut the door behind him and affording Destiny the sight of Derek's personal assistant, a woman in her mid-fifties, hurriedly half-rising as Callum swept past her, the expression on her flushed face one of addled confusion.

By the time she arrived at the company, Destiny was feeling addled and confused herself. Over lunch—an intricately arranged fresh tuna salad, the sight of which had nearly made her burst out laughing, so remotely had it resembled anything edible—she had tried to find out a bit more about the much-maligned directors she was to meet. But Derek had not been a source of useful information. His friendship with her uncle stretched back a long way and there was a debt of gratitude to him which ensured his unswerving loyalty. Fighting hard not to be distracted by the comings and goings in the restaurant, she'd discovered that Abraham Felt had helped Derek when he had first struck out, decades previously, on his own. No wonder he was so protective of her and so unofficially antagonistic towards Callum Ross!

Walking into the glass monument to wealth further shredded her nerves.

'You'll get used to it,' Derek murmured staunchly at her side, as they got into the elevator and glided up to the third floor. Destiny doubted it.

'You wouldn't say that if you were in my shoes,' she murmured back, thinking that *in my sandals* would have been a more appropriate description. Three months previously she and her father had made the nine-hour trek to Panama City and had spent two days shopping for essentials, but somehow London was a great deal more daunting than the country she had learnt to love. However, come hell or high water, she would buy some clothes in the morning. Derek had established a bank account for her and she had arrived in England with more money than she had seen in a lifetime at her immediate disposal. Whether she liked it or not, she would have to get rid of her ethnic garb and conform.

'You don't have to say anything if you don't want to,' Derek told her, as the elevator doors slid open. 'Just get a feel for the people, for the company. You already know what the state of their profit and loss column looks like, so to speak, but you can put it all into real perspective once you've met the people in charge.'

Four hours later, Destiny thought that that was easier said than done. All the directors had been there, except the one she was most curious to meet, her stepcousin, and their reactions had run the gamut from suspicion, to relief that she had not summarily announced that she would be selling, to wheedling as they brought out their individual reports and regaled her with why she shouldn't abandon the ship.

They were all men in their late fifties, on the verge of retirement, and she'd inappropriately recalled Callum's scathing description of them as a pack of old fools when Tim Headley had patted her hand and attempted to excuse four years of misguided management under the heading of 'going through a bad patch.'

'I shall go home and read all this,' she had said wearily, as three o'clock had rolled into four, then five, then six. It had been a further hour and a half before she had finally managed to leave and had been told by a beaming Derek that she had *done really well. Buoyed them up. Given them that little injection of hope they needed.*

Her head was throbbing when she at last made it back to her house, for which she felt an inordinate rush of fondness as it contained the two things she wanted most. A well-stocked fridge and a bed.

She'd not managed to attack the first when her telephone rang and she heard a breathless, girlish voice down the end of the line.

'Who *is* this?' she demanded, cradling the telephone between shoulder and head as she fumbled to undo the front fastening buttons of her dress.

'Stephanie. I should have been at the meeting this afternoon, but…somehow my appointments overran…'

Destiny stopped what she was doing and held the telephone properly.

'Anyway, I thought that perhaps we could meet for supper this evening? You could come to my apartment— actually, I only live about ten minutes' drive away from you…?'

'Well…' The thought of slotting in one more piece of the jigsaw puzzle that had become her life was too enticing to resist. 'If you tell me where you are…can I walk to you? No?… How do I get a taxi?… Yes, right… Well, give me about forty-five minutes and I'll be there… Right, yes, that's fine… Yes, I *do* know what Chinese food consists of… Okay, fine, bye.'

As she inspected her wardrobe, selecting the least colourful of her dresses, she wondered what her stepcousin would be like. Her gut feeling warned her that a disaster lay ahead. Callum Ross was made of steel and any fiancée of his would more than likely be made of similar stuff. She was fast developing a healthy streak of cynicism in this bewildering world where scheming seemed to be part of an acceptable game and exploitation was part and parcel of the same game. The healthy streak of cynicism was now telling her that Stephanie Felt had probably been primed by her lover to use every trick in the book to get what she wanted. Her healthy streak of cynicism was going one step further and warning her that the other woman had probably avoided the meeting on purpose, simply so that their first meeting could be on her own territory. Alone. Destiny stared back dejectedly at her reflection in the bathroom mirror and discovered that, despite her lifelong predilection for all things logical and scientific, her imagination was scrabbling frantically now to make up for lost time.

She left the townhouse nervous, but grimly resolved to face down yet one more enemy. The taxi carried her out of Knightsbridge and into the heart of Chelsea, and then stopped in front of a Victorian house, one in a row of many, all of which were as impeccably maintained as the one she had just left.

She sighed involuntarily as she rang the doorbell. Her nervous system couldn't take much more. She longed with a physical ache for the simplicity of her compound, with its heat and wild beauty and unthreatening routines.

From Callum Ross to Stephanie Felt in the space of a few short hours. She wondered what else could hit her. There must be some evil, as yet undisclosed relation somewhere in the background, clutching a potion, a broomstick and a book of spells.

The woman who answered the door almost made her gasp in surprise.

'Hiya.' More of a girl than a woman, just out of her teens from the look of it, with wavy brown hair and huge blue eyes. Even in her heels, she was still small. Small and slender, her heartshaped face smoothly unlined by time.

'Have I come to the right house?' Destiny blustered, trying to peer at the plaque on the door to see whether she had made a mistake with the numbers. 'I'm looking for Stephanie Felt.'

'That's me.' When she smiled, her face dimpled and she stood back to let Destiny walk past. 'I've been dying to meet you, you know. *A stepcousin!* I never even *knew* you existed until Callum told me! Can you believe it? Abraham never mentioned his family, not even to Mum!' Her voice was light and excited as she led the way to the sitting room. 'You'll have to tell me all about where you lived. I've never been to your part of the world—never. Can you believe it? Callum says it's really primitive where you come from. Gosh!' She turned around and looked at Destiny with glowing curiosity and awe. 'This must all seem very strange to you! I love your dress, by the way. Neat. All those swirly colours. Is that what the people over there wear? Is it, like, their native costume, so to speak?'

'No, not really.' Destiny smiled. For the first time since she had set foot on English shores, she felt unthreatened and relaxed. 'Most of the women in the Indian tribes I come into contact with walk around bare-breasted...'

'Which would never do,' came a familiar drawling voice, 'so I should practise that mode of dress only in the privacy of your own house.'

Sure enough, Callum was sprawled in a chair strategically positioned so that Destiny was afforded a full-frontal of the man at leisure. It was the first time she had seen him without the formality of a suit and she was taken aback to realise that he looked younger. Younger yet no less off-putting. His cream trousers made his legs seem longer and the short-sleeved shirt with the top two buttons undone revealed masculine forearms and a sneak preview of dark hair shadowing his chest.

Her mouth felt disconcertingly dry and she almost shrieked her, 'Yes, please!' when Stephanie offered her something to drink. 'Beer, please.'

'Beer?' they both echoed in unison, with varying degrees of surprise on their faces.

'Perhaps not.' She faltered and looked to her stepcousin for support.

'Perhaps some wine?' Stephanie suggested, grinning. 'It's nice and cold.'

'Yes, thank you, that sounds fine.' She breathed a sigh of relief and sat down in the chair facing Callum, more because of its relative proximity than for any other reason, although the badly chosen seating arrangement now guaranteed an uninterrupted vision of him.

'You were talking about your national costume—or, rather, the lack of it,' he said, crossing his extended legs at the ankles and linking his fingers together on his lap.

'What are you doing here?' Destiny surprised herself by asking. This man, like it or not, made her say things and behave in ways that were alien to her. And her skin felt hot and itchy under the intensity of his blue eyes. Was that possible? Could someone make someone else feel hot and itchy just by looking at them? It had certainly never happened to her before.

His eyebrows shot up in exaggerated astonishment at her question. 'Stephanie's my fiancée. Naturally I wanted to be by her side when she met her stepcousin for the first time. She's a very gentle soul.' He lowered his eyes when he said this but there was a tell-tale smile tugging the corners of his mouth. 'I didn't want you to terrify her.'

'*Me? Terrify her?*' Her protesting voice was more of a furious splutter.

'With your aggression.'

'*My aggression?* How can you talk about *my* aggression?'

She reduced the volume of her voice at the sound of approaching footsteps, but the rankled feeling managed to stay with her for the remainder of the evening. Even more infuriating was the fact that her fulminating looks did very little more than provide him with a source of barely contained amusement.

Only Stephanie's cheerful banter, as she dragged out details of Panama from her guest, besieging her with interested questions, squealing with delight when Destiny talked about the children she taught and gasping with little cries of horror at her stories of the jungle and what it contained, saved the evening. Destiny wondered if her stepcousin knew that she would be marrying someone who made the most ferocious jungle animal pale in comparison.

They had spoken not one word of business by the time eleven-thirty rolled around and she stood to leave, feeling woozy from the wine, to which she was in no way accustomed, and exhausted by her jet lag.

'So, what did you make of the buffoons at the company?' Callum asked, standing up as well and shoving his hands into his pockets. 'I suppose they pulled out all the stops? Made you pore over cobwebbed reports of how great and good the firm used to be years ago? Played down what a shambles it's in now?' Despite consuming what had seemed, to Destiny, prodigious amounts of wine during the evening, the man still looked bright-eyed, alert and rearing to attack.

She threw him a wilted looked and stifled a yawn.

'Mmm. *That* interesting, was it?' A wicked glint of humour shone in his eyes.

'I wasn't trying to make a comment on what the meeting was like,' Destiny said with lukewarm protest in her voice. 'I'm tired.'

'Leave her alone, Callum,' Stephanie said sympathetically.

'Business has to be discussed, Steph.'

'Why now? It's so boring.'

'Boring for *you* perhaps, but you want to remember that your finances are tied up with what happens next in this little exciting scenario. I buy the company, play with it a bit until it's running along smoothly, and *your* shares go up. Our Panamanian heiress keeps the company and—'

'Do you mind *not* talking as if I wasn't here?'

'Have you ever been to London before, Destiny?' Stephanie linked her arm through her stepcousin's and ushered her to the front door, pointedly turning her back on her fiancée.

'No. It's all new and—' she glanced over her shoulder and her eyes clashed with Callum's '—a little scary.'

'It would be. You're just so brave to come all this way, on your own. I'd never dream of doing it!'

'No.' Callum's voice behind them was silky. 'It takes a certain type of woman to do that. Some might call it brave, darling; others might just call it—well, let's just say that it's a very *masculine* response.'

At which Stephanie flew around to face him with her hands on her hips and a simmering look in her baby-blue eyes. 'Don't be *horrible!*'

'Me?' He raised both his hands in innocent denial, but the blue eyes that locked with Destiny's were unrepentant. 'Horrible? It was meant to be a *compliment!* A glorious example of how far the women's movement has got!'

'What women's movement?' Destiny asked, her body language echoing Stephanie's. 'I've never been a part of any movement in my life before!'

'No?' He tried to stifle a grin and failed miserably. 'Well, let's just say that feminism has missed out there.'

'Meaning what?'

'Meaning that I'll give you a lift back to your place.'
He bent over to give Stephanie a gentlemanly peck on
the cheek and a pat on the back. 'That all right with you,
darling?'

'Don't badger her, Callum.'

'I wish people wouldn't constantly stereotype me.' He
pulled open the front door and gave Destiny an exagger-
atedly wide berth to exit ahead of him into a clear night
that was considerably more bracing than it had been ear-
lier on in the evening.

'What about tomorrow?' Stephanie asked him, standing in the doorway to see them off, an angelic, diminutive
shape that made Destiny feel like an Amazonian hulk in
comparison. 'The Holts have invited us to supper. Did
you remember? Daisy and Clarence are going to be there
as well. Oh, and Rupert.'

Callum paused and frowned, appearing to give the
matter weighty thought, then he said with a shrug,

'Meeting. Sorry, darling. You go, though. Don't stay
in because of me.'

'You're *always* at meetings,' Stephanie said in a child-
ish, sulky voice. 'He's *always* at meetings,' she addressed
Destiny in an appeal to sisterhood, which Destiny took
up with sadistic relish.

'If he loved you, he'd cancel, I'm sure.'

'If you loved me, you'd cancel.'

There was a brief silence. 'I'll do my best.' He sighed
and Stephanie's face radiated at this unexpected victory.

'Oh, goody!' She blew them both a delighted kiss and
shut the front door on them.

CHAPTER THREE

'THANK you. Thank you very much,' he grated sarcastically, as the engine of his powerful car purred into life. He pulled away from the kerb unnecessarily fast and Destiny clutched the car door handle to steady herself.

In the shadows of the car, his averted profile was hard and unsmiling and she had to stifle a desire to burst out laughing. Suddenly, sleep was no longer beckoning at her door. In fact, she felt surprisingly revived, and wondered whether her body might not just have been craving some fresh air.

Not that the London air was particularly fresh. Back in Panama, when she breathed in, she could smell everything. The musky aroma of hot, hard-packed dirt, the rich fullness of the trees and the bushes, the distant freshness of the snake-like river coiling its way lazily into the heart of the jungle. At certain times during the day she could smell the fragrance of food being cooked. Sometimes, when she closed her eyes, she could almost seem to detect the smells of the sky and the clouds and the stillness.

Here, she felt stuffy. Pollution, of course. Not as severe as she had seen in Mexico years ago, where the pollution bordered on contamination, but there nevertheless, unseen but ever-present.

'Thank you for what?' she asked innocently, playing him at his own game, and his mouth turned down darkly at the corners.

'You *know* what for,' he accused, looking away briefly from the empty road to glare at her. 'I'd hoped Stephanie

44

had forgotten all about that damned dinner party. Now I'm going to have to go and spend at least three agonising hours being bored to death by Rupert and his cronies.'

'Oh, dear,' she said unsympathetically, which provoked another blistering look.

'Where,' he asked, 'did you get that?'

'Get what?' Her voice was genuinely surprised.

'Your sarcasm. I always thought that missionaries were supposed to be glucose-sweet.'

Destiny bristled. 'I am *not* a missionary, actually. If you'd done your homework properly, you might have discovered *why* we're on a compound in the heart of Panama, and it has nothing to do with converting anyone to any kind of religion. We're there to help educate people in desperate need of education, and I'm not really talking about reading, writing and arithmetic.'

'What, then?' He could feel himself reluctantly being drawn in, like a fish on the end of a line, curious to find out details of the background that had produced the creature sitting next to him. It felt peculiar to find himself hanging on to a woman's conversation when normally he was the one playing the conversational game, digging into his reserves of wit and charm without even realising it. He wasn't sure whether he liked it or not. He felt himself relax his foot on the accelerator so that the car meandered along.

'We teach them how to use the land they have to maximise their crops—how to be self-sufficient, in other words. We help them with distributing crafts. Some of them make things for the tourist market in the city. And naturally we teach them the usual stuff.'

'*We?*'

'Yes. All of us. We work together. I'm a qualified doctor, but I'm also responsible for the formal classes.

Of course, we have specialists on the compound as well. Not just the children need education; so do the adults. How to use their resources to their best advantage, how to rotate certain crops so that the land is never unused. How to take advantage of the rains when they come. Our agricultural expert is responsible for that side of things, but we all chip in.'

'Like one big happy family.'

Destiny narrowed her eyes on him, but she couldn't read his expression and his voice was mild.

'Something like that.'

'Cosy.'

'Yes, it is. Why are you driving so slowly? I want to get back.'

Callum pressed his foot marginally harder on the accelerator and muttered something inconsequential about speed limits, fines and points on a driving licence.

'What points?'

'Never mind. It doesn't matter.' He felt his jaw begin to ache and realised that he was clenching his teeth. 'So what do you do on those long, balmy evenings, anyway? On your compound?'

'*Long, balmy evenings?* It's not a seaside resort.'

'No, of course not.' Clenching again. He relaxed his jaw muscles and realised, with a twinge of disappointment, that her house was now within view. The guard barely glanced at them. He just waved them through and he pulled up very slowly in front of her house.

'Thank you very much,' Destiny said, fiddling with the seat belt and finally releasing it. 'It was lovely to meet Stephanie. I'm sorry if you think that it's my fault that you're going to have dinner with some boring friends tomorr—'

'Oh, forget it.' He waved aside her apologies irritably

and watched as she walked up to the front door. For a tall girl, she was surprisingly agile, graceful even. She'd never answered his question about what she spent her evenings doing, he realised. He waited, watching as various lights were turned on and switched off, tracing her progress through the house, even though he couldn't see a thing because the curtains were all drawn. When the place was in darkness, he impulsively got out of his car, sprinted up to the front door and insistently buzzed the bell, keeping his finger on the button until he heard the sounds of shuffling behind the door.

This time Destiny looked through the peep hole and reluctantly opened the door. 'What do you want *now?*'

'It's that damned car,' he said, raking his fingers through his hair and casting an accusing look in the direction of the inert lump of silver metal on the road. 'Won't start.'

'*What?*' She'd pulled on a robe over her long, baggy tee-shirt which served as a nightgown, and now she clutched it tighter around her as she continued to eye him with mounting dismay.

What now? She didn't want him in her house! When he wasn't getting on her nerves he was getting under her skin, and she had enough to cope with without Callum Ross sending her normally well-behaved nervous system into overdrive.

He shook his head and then glanced at her. 'I wouldn't have bothered you... You hadn't got into bed as yet, had you?'

'About to.'

'Well, I wouldn't have troubled you, but it's given up on me and I need to use a phone.'

'A phone? At *this* hour? Who are you going to phone

to fix your car at *this hour?* Do car mechanics work around the clock over here?'

'If I could just come in—it's a bit nippy out here…'

For a few seconds she didn't look as though she was going to budge, but then she reluctantly stepped back and he slipped past her just in case she changed her mind and slammed the door in his face.

'It seemed to be working perfectly fine on the drive over.' Destiny stood where she was and folded her arms.

'Ah, yes. That's the problem, you see. I've been meaning to get it seen to for the past week or so, but I haven't managed to find a spare moment…to book it in to a garage. Didn't you notice that it was going particularly slowly on the way over here?'

Destiny inclined her head to one side and remained silent.

'One minute it's absolutely fine; the next minute it's losing power.' He cleared his throat and attempted to take firm control of the proceedings instead of acting like a schoolboy caught doing something underhand. Smoking behind the bicycle shed.

'The telephone's behind you.'

'Ah, good. Good, good, good.' He lifted the receiver and dialled his driver. He felt a heel, actually, having to rouse the man from a deep sleep, but whoever said that life was fair? 'Bennet's coming over as soon as he gets dressed. Might be half an hour or so.' He wondered whether she'd heard him murmuring indistinctly into the phone that there was no rush, within the hour would be fine. 'Don't let me keep you from bed… You pop along…I'll stay down here. The family silver's safe.'

Destiny clicked her tongue in annoyance and headed towards the kitchen. 'I might as well make you a cup of coffee,' she offered grudgingly.

'Don't put yourself out,' he said, following her and then lounging comfortably on one of the kitchen chairs while she filled the kettle and fetched two mugs down from a cupboard. 'Although,' he said pensively, 'you *do* owe me a favour after your trapping me into tomorrow night's hilarity.'

'I had no idea that seeing your fiancée was a trap.' She pelted a spoonful of instant into each of the mugs, sloshed some boiling water in and topped it off with milk.

'Stephanie isn't the problem.' He hooked out another chair with his foot and proceeded to stretch both legs out in front of him and watch her with his hands behind his head. 'Her friends are the problem. The women titter and giggle and the men talk in booming voices and compare drinking anecdotes.' Despite her attempts to cover herself, her robe slipped open as she handed him his mug of coffee and he was privy to the sight of her long body encased in the least attractive item of clothing he could think of seeing on a woman. A faded and well-worn tee-shirt hanging to her knees with some barely identifiable advertising motif on the front.

She sat down opposite him and blew on the surface of her coffee. 'How long will this car mechanic be?'

'I told him to get here as quickly as possible. Believe me, the last thing I need now is to be sitting here at the ungodly hour of midnight, waiting for someone to come and fix my car. With work tomorrow.' He ferociously gulped a mouthful of coffee. 'And another late night on the horizon.' He looked at her speculatively. 'Why don't you come along?'

'Come along where?' For one bizarre moment she thought he was inviting her to go to work with him.

'Come along to the little dinner party I'm being dragged to? Stephanie would be thrilled and you could meet some people.' He lowered his eyes and sipped some more coffee. 'There'll probably be one or two eligible men there...' He let the offer fall into the silence like a stone dropping into a pond. 'Unless, of course, you're already involved with someone...' He risked a quick look to see how this was registering. 'Someone out there in Panama?'

'That's none of your business.'

'Merely trying to introduce you to a social life.'

'I'm here to sort things out with the company,' Destiny said shortly. 'And then I shall be heading back home. I don't *need* a social life, thank you.'

'Everyone needs a social life. Don't tell me you don't enjoy some kind of social life out there. On that compound of yours.' He tried to imagine it and failed. 'You're a young woman, after all.'

'How long have you and my stepcousin been engaged?'

There was no attempt to disguise the change of topic and Callum cursed under his breath. 'Two years.'

'Two years! And you're not married yet?'

'It's hardly shocking,' he said with a trace of impatience in his voice. He had never considered it a long time. In fact, even now, there were no plans for a wedding on the horizon. Neither he nor Stephanie was particularly adamant on moving the step further. 'Marriage is a serious business. What's the point rushing into it? You know what they say about marrying in haste and repenting at leisure.'

'Yes, but if you're certain about someone, then why hang around?' She rested her elbow on the table and cupped her chin in one hand while the other cradled her mug, idly stroking the ceramic surface as she continued to look at him.

'Two years is hardly *hanging around.*' Silence. 'Is it?' Further silence. 'It's nothing to do with whether you've found the right person or not.' Was it particularly hot in the kitchen? He was perspiring and he ran one finger under the collar of his shirt. 'Marriage is little more than a piece of paper anyway.'

'I thought you said that it was a serious business.'

'This is a ridiculous conversation. I was simply inviting you out to meet a few people and rescue you from the prospect of spending your nights cooped up in this place.' Alarmingly, he could detect pique in his voice. 'Through the goodness of my heart.'

At that, she raised her eyebrows in patent disbelief and he gave her a thunderous look. 'The goodness of your heart? You haven't *got* a heart! You want to buy my company and that's all that interests you! I'm a spoke in your wheel and you would do anything to get rid of it!'

'That's business,' he muttered. 'The fact is, that whether we like it or not, I'm engaged to your stepcousin, so we're going to see one another in the course of things.'

'How can you separate business from pleasure? How can you treat someone one way when you're sitting across a desk from them and then treat them completely differently when you're sitting across a dinner table?'

'Why can't you just accept what's handed to you and not read ulterior motives behind everything?'

'You're the one who showed up at this house unannounced,' she pointed out, 'so that you could try and wheedle me into selling you the company before I'd had time to see the directors or even take advice from Derek.'

'I was not trying to wheedle you into selling anything!' Callum exploded. He stood up and began savagely pacing the kitchen.

'Why don't you just help me get the company into

shape?' she demanded. 'That would be a good solution. And you would still have some shares in it through Stephanie.'

At this, he gave a snort of derisory laughter. 'What, you mean pour some of my own money into your company, money I would never get back? Why the hell would I do that?'

'What would you do with the company if I *did* agree to sell it to you?' She could feel her own thought processes getting agitated and jerky. Her eyes compulsively followed him as he prowled, soaking up his expressive hands, the hard, good-looking face with its sensual, curving mouth.

'Make it a working proposition.'

'Don't you mean chop it up into sections and sell it off individually once it's up and running?'

'Which only shows your ignorance of the facts!' he snapped back at her. 'I intend to incorporate it into my own portfolio.'

'And what about the people who work there?' she demanded.

'Most would stay. Some would be asked to leave.'

'Who? *Who* would you ask to leave?'

'I'm not about to hand over that kind of information to you.'

'Why not?'

'Because we're on opposite sides of the fence!' He realised that he was on the verge of shouting. He was a man who couldn't remember the last time he had raised his voice, because so much more could be achieved with a murmur—yet here he was, practically shouting. He was also breathing hard and fast, as though he had just completed a marathon. 'You,' he grated, approaching her chair, scraping it around so that he was staring down at her, 'are impossible.' He leaned over her, his hands on either side of her chair, caging her in so that she was forced backwards as though the pressure of his personality was a physical force. 'In fact, I would go so far as to say that *you* are the most impossible woman I have *ever* met in my entire life!' His face was inches away from hers and Destiny was suddenly terrified. Not terrified that he might hit her, or even hurl another well-targeted insult at her. She was terrified because something in what he said struck deep into her and caused her pain. The backs of her eyes began to sting and she blinked furiously.

'That's not very kind,' she whispered in a small voice, and then, to her further dismay, a lonesome tear trickled down her cheek. She brushed it aside in a wave of mortification and stared down at her fingers.

'Oh, God. Don't do that. Please don't do that. Here.' He fumbled in his pocket and extracted a handkerchief. 'Take this.'

Destiny blindly grabbed it and wiped her eyes, pressing her fingers into them to staunch any further leakage.

'I'm sorry,' he said roughly. 'I didn't think… Oh, God, say something, would you…? Please?'

She would, she thought, if she could, but she knew better than to rely on her vocal cords right now. Instead, she twisted the handkerchief in her fingers, playing with it for distraction from the appalling situation she was now in.

'I'm sorry, Destiny. I never dreamt…'

'It's all right,' she said on a sigh. 'Would you mind…? I can't breathe with you so close…'

Callum swiftly withdrew, but only to drag a chair in front of hers, which gave her a reprieve of several inches more but not enough.

'Look,' she said in a steadier voice, 'there's no need to apologise. I know I'm not…not what men…' She paused and sucked in her breath, then expelled it a little shakily. 'I realise that I'm not feminine and frilly and the sort of woman that men…I've never known what it was like to date boys and flirt.' A fleeting glance at a face that was far too concerned for her comfort, then some more frantic twisting of the handkerchief. 'I mean, my lifestyle has taught me how to be strong. I've always had to be, you see. Weakness isn't something that goes down too well when you're in the middle of nowhere and someone might be depending on you to administer medicine to them or sew some stitches or draw out toxin from a snake bite.'

He stroked her hair, running his fingers through it in a soothing, rhythmic way.

'You should try looking in the mirror some time,' he murmured.

'Not many of them are long enough to fit all of me in.' She tried an unsuccessful laugh and thought with a certain amount of envy of her stepcousin. *She* was the sort of woman oozing feminine attraction. Soft and small and girlishly sexy. There was nothing feigned about her and nature had kindly lent her a huge helping hand at birth in the form of a tiny, neat body and the kind of face that would always have men running behind her like lap-dogs. Big, strong men like the one in front of her now. She'd read enough articles in magazines about men and their need to act as protector to their women. Not too many about men who liked women who could protect themselves and at a pinch could probably do a passable job at protecting *them* in the bargain.

Perhaps she should just sell the damned company and head back to where she belonged. This big, new world was too big for her. She felt like the country mouse on its ruinous trip to visit the town mouse.

The sound of the doorbell clanged into the brief silence between them and she jumped as though she had been scalded. He started as well and muttered an oath under his breath; then he stood up and waited till she had risen shakily to her feet.

Relief washed over her. She was not one for spouting forth confidences. When it came to her thoughts and her feelings, Destiny was adept at keeping her counsel. She could scarcely believe that Callum Ross had somehow broken through her reserve and extracted depths of self-pity which she'd never known even existed.

Now, she just wanted him out. She practically shovelled him to the front door.

'Are you sure you won't come with us tomorrow evening?' he asked, taking his time even though he must be able to sense her urgency to get rid of him.

'Quite sure.'

'When do you expect to come to a decision about the company?'

Destiny shrugged, back in control of her wayward feelings. 'I'm spending a week there going through things with the directors and Derek; then I'm going to talk to the accountant and try and get an honest opinion of whether the company's salvageable or not.'

'It's not, without a huge injection of capital—which you haven't got. You don't have to talk to your accountant for that information. You can just talk to me.'

'I hope to have come to some kind of decision once I've done that,' she carried on, ignoring his interruption. She reached out to open the front door and he grasped her wrist. Her eyes, he noticed, were still pink, even though her voice was steady. She had lost control and he sensed that she had surprised herself. Surprised herself because she was not a woman who frequently lost control or resorted to any feminine wiles such as the random shedding of tears to stir the heartstrings. For a minute she'd allowed him into her world, and he could taste his own desire to find out more like a drug coursing through his veins.

Her wrist caught between his fingers felt hot and his breathing was sluggish.

'Would you mind letting me go?' Her green eyes were polite and cautious, and for a second he wondered how she would react if he told her that he really *would* mind.

'Why don't we meet over dinner to discuss details of…the company?' he said. He edged towards the door, opened it slightly and nodded to his driver. 'Hate getting you out here at this ungodly hour but it won't do a thing, George. Completely useless piece of machinery. Give it a go, would you?' His hand was still gripping hers.

'There's nothing to discuss until—'

'I want to show you some of the plans I have for the company, should you sell.'

'Could you let me go, please?'

He obediently dropped her hand but remained strategically placed in front of the door, which he had quietly shut back.

'Dinner tomorrow night. I'll pick you up around seven thirty.'

'I have no intent—'

'It's really a good idea to get all your facts in place before you make any kind of decision.'

'Derek—'

'—has no say whatsoever in your decision. He might want to puff himself out and hold your hand but there's no need for you to stroke his ego by going along for the ride...'

'I'm doing no such thing!'

'No? Sure? No girlish, helpless giggles while he pontificates and throws his weight around?'

'I am not a *helpless, giggling girl*,' Destiny informed him hotly.

'Then why are you so afraid of meeting me without him around as a chaperon?'

'I am *not afraid of meeting you*,' she said through gritted teeth.

'Good. Then tomorrow at seven thirty.'

'And what would Stephanie say to that?'

'I'm proposing a meeting to discuss business,' Callum interjected smoothly, gratified to see a tell-tale flush spread across her face. He savoured it for a few seconds, then continued, 'I'm sure she wouldn't have any objections.'

'My wardrobe is a bit scant,' Destiny objected weakly. Had she just been bulldozed into something? It certainly felt like it although, when she recapped their conversation, she couldn't pinpoint *why*.

'You're going shopping tomorrow, though.'

'Oh, so I am. And how do you know that, anyway?'

'You mentioned it to Stephanie over dinner.'

For someone who had not seemed highly riveted at the time, the man had a keen listening ear, she thought.

'You should take her along with you. I know she'd be thrilled. There's very little Steph appreciates more than several hours spent tramping in and out of stores and spending money like water.'

'In which case, I'd better not.' An involuntary smile flitted across her face. 'If there's one thing *I* don't appreciate, it's tramping in and out of stores. I wouldn't know about the *spending money like water,* having never had any, but I suspect I probably wouldn't much like that either.'

There was the sound of the car revving into action, which galvanised Callum into yanking open the door and, before his driver could say a word, she was mystified to see him spoken to in low undertones and then Callum was in the passenger seat and the car was gliding away into the night.

Leaving her, she thought the following morning, facing yet another stressful encounter with a man whose image was proving to have superglue properties when it came to lodging in her head.

Despite that, when, just as she was about to leave the house, her father called, she found herself reluctant to confide anything about Callum. It was the first time she had spoken to him since she'd arrived in England, and he'd had to go to the nearest town for use of a telephone. He told her everything that was happening on the compound, little titbits of gossip that made her smile, passed on a *missing you* message from Henri, and conjured up pictures of heat and jungle that seemed more than a lifetime away. In return, she told him what she had been up to, downplaying her own feelings of inadequacy at being thrown in at the deep end to cope with a situation for which nothing in her life had prepared her. She tried to make London sound exciting, because she knew that her father would worry himself sick if she did otherwise, but really when she thought about London the image became entangled with the image of Callum—whose presence she diluted, for her father's benefit, into *an annoying little man who wants me to sell the company.*

'Don't be bullied into doing anything you don't want to do,' her father said anxiously.

'Oh, I can take care of myself, Dad,' Destiny said. 'I'm not worried at all by Callum Ross.' She conjured up a mental picture of his dark, powerful face, and said with a grin, 'He's really just a silly little chap who thinks he can get his own way.'

'Sounds an unpleasant type, my darling. Why don't you let that Derek man take care of him?'

'Oh, I can handle the man myself,' she said airily.

'Eat him up and spit him out,' her father said with a smile in his voice, which was a compliment, she knew, but managed to reignite those niggling little ideas that had taken root in her mind ever since she had met Callum Ross. Little ideas that being fiercely independent and being able to take care of herself was all very well in the depths of Panama, but somehow out of place in a city where the interaction between the opposite sexes called for an appealing helplessness that she found difficult to muster. In fact, impossible.

She hung up after fifteen minutes, feeling vaguely depressed. She looked in the mirror and saw an ill-dressed, unfeminine, overtall and utterly unsexy woman with hair chopped into no particular cut and a body too well toned by a life that had always involved physical exertion. She had no problem kayaking along treacherous rivers through dense undergrowth, but there were no treacherous rivers in the city of London and that particular talent was useless. She had no use for make-up in the steaming heat, but here her face felt naked. The clothes she had always worn, loose-fitting and functional, were fine on the compound, but she was fast realising that dressing sensibly to cope with heat and mosquitoes was good in the jungle but depressingly laughable in a city. Her hands, strong and hard-working, now seemed like hands a man should have and not a woman.

Had she forgotten somewhere along the way that she *was* a woman? The thought made her even more dejected. She thought of her stepcousin with her beautifully manicured nails painted the pink of candy floss and felt graceless and gauche in comparison.

Henri thinks that I'm attractive, she thought to herself. But did he really? Or did he just think that she was the best of the bunch?

Five hours spent on Oxford Street and the King's Road was no sop to her deflated spirits. She spent a great deal of time wondering which shops were worth visiting and looking around her in a bewildered, confused fashion. Several times she had literally been swept along by the crowds of shoppers like a tadpole caught in a downstream current.

The pace was swift and left no room for uncertain young girls with no particular agenda aside from gathering the skeleton of a wardrobe together.

In the end, she found herself outside Harvey Nichols, took a deep breath and handed herself over to the experience of a shop assistant. She did her best not to convert the vast quantities of money she was spending on clothes into an amount that would have bought a lot more important things in Panama.

She bought two skirts and jackets that would do for when she went into the company to work, jeans and shirts and jumpers for casual wear, and shoes that made her feet feel ten sizes smaller and looked, to her unaccustomed eyes, positively ludicrous. She threw caution to the winds and indulged in lingerie that wasn't sensible. She allowed herself to be persuaded into two dresses which, the shop assistant assured her were perfect, with a firmness that defied contradiction—especially from someone who had no idea what might or might not suit her.

'But they're tight,' Destiny protested weakly, looking at the black dress and the deep green dress with concern. Tight clothes were anathema in blistering heat and she had never possessed anything that clung. Least of all clung to her curves. 'And they're short.'

'They're sexy,' the shop assistant explained, casting a critical eye over her victim and pushing her towards a changing booth.

Destiny emerged feeling like a tree inappropriately clad in a bikini, but when she looked in the mirror she realised with a twinge of pleasure that she was nothing like a tree. Tall, yes, but slim and with curves that had rarely seen the light of day.

Her legs seemed to stretch on and on and on, long and brown and slender, and her breasts, not camouflaged by baggy clothes, jutted out provocatively.

'Of course, you should get your hair cut into something fashionable,' she was told.

It was shoulder-length, and years of DIY home cuts had lent it a rough, uneven edge, all the more apparent because it was so incredibly blonde.

'I like my hair,' Destiny said. 'I'm not going to have it short.' Back in her work gear in Panama, stripped of these wildly glamorous plumes that seemed to turn her into a sexy woman, of sorts, and with a cropped haircut, she really would look like one of the men. No chance. Her mother had always insisted that she have some length to her hair and she wasn't about to abandon that piece of advice now.

But buy the clothes she did. The whole lot. She also bought make-up, which took ages because the choice of colours and shades of everything almost defied belief. At the end of it, the shopping bags seemed as heavy to carry back to the house as a dozen bags of medicine, school-books, containers of plant specimens and the kayak rolled into one.

It was worth it, though.

She knew that when, at seven-thirty, she looked at her reflection and what gazed back at her was a striking woman in a short, tight black dress, wearing smart black, albeit hideously uncomfortable, shoes and a face that was a blend of subtle colours. Blushing Pink on her lips, which made her tan stand out, a hint of Passionate Petal blusher and length enhancing mascara that made her eye-lashes look as though they had taken growth hormones.

She would not give Callum Ross another opportunity to sneer at her for being *impossible*—which really boiled down to *unfeminine*.

She wasn't dressing for him, she insisted to herself, but neither was she going to be treated like someone whose lack of sophistication was an excuse for insults. She had no idea how long she would be in London—two weeks, three, maybe more—and while she was here she would damn well change her colours to match her sur-roundings. Animals did it and so could she.

CHAPTER FOUR

DESTINY felt a surge of disproportionate disappointment when she opened the door to Callum, bursting with smug satisfaction at the figure she presented, and was greeted merely with, 'Oh, good. You're ready. I can't stand waiting around for a woman to get her act together.'

She slammed the door behind her and preceded him to the car. 'Did you bring whatever paperwork you wanted me to have a look at?' One minute he was full of scathing asides on her appearance and inability to cope with life in the fast track, and then, when she *did* make an effort, she noticed petulantly, he didn't even have the good grace to comment on it!

'In the car.' His eyes flicked rapidly over her as she folded herself into the car seat and he added perfunctorily, 'Had a successful day shopping, then, I take it?'

'Very successful, thank you.'

He looked away, turned the key in the ignition and the powerful car roared into life.

'And not too much useless tramping in and out of stores?' he quizzed her with the ghost of a smile on his mouth.

Destiny, pressed against the car door, attempted to compose her features into a mask of unrevealing politeness. If he had the slightest idea how much his opinion meant to her, she had no doubt that he would ruthlessly use the knowledge to get what he wanted.

'Quite a bit of useless tramping in and out of stores, actually.' He was wearing a plain-coloured shirt with some logo almost invisibly embroidered on the front pocket, and dark trousers. She could feel herself going into an undignified trance as she feasted her eyes on him, and with a little twinge of guilt she dragged them away and stared out of the window. She was already beginning to get used to the fact that no part of London was free from crowds. Even at this hour of the evening there seemed to be no let-up from the hordes of people in search of open shops and entertainment. Did no one sleep here? she wondered.

'Mmm. To be expected, considering you don't know where to go. You should have listened to me and gone along with Steph.'

'Does *she* always listen to you?'

'Most people do,' he said comfortably.

'Would that be because you're a bully?'

He frowned at her, and his brief lapse in concentration caused him to brake suddenly behind the black cab in front.

'Could you try not to distract me when I'm driving? London is a bloody obstacle course. The last thing I need is for the two of us to land up in hospital.'

'Which would be *my* fault because I'm trying to make polite conversation?'

'Telling me that I'm a bully is your way of making polite conversation? I don't run around yelling at people and telling them what to do and how to live their lives. I'm very reasonable and usually right.'

'Oh.'

Next to her, Callum simmered silently, barely seeing the crowds overflowing the pavements as they drove through the busy theatre district. He dared not keep his foot on the accelerator and risk another glance at her without opening himself up to a possible crash, but he was itching to. He wasn't idiotic or egotistical enough to imagine that she had put on that sexy little black number for his benefit, but it was having a roller-coaster effect on his senses. Dressed like that, she even *smelt* more womanly. The neckline was scooped and cut low enough to reveal the swelling roundness of her breasts. Not even the thought of Stephanie, with her childishly boyish figure, was enough to put a brake on his wandering imagination. It wasn't disloyalty, he told himself sternly. It was a natural male response to look at a beautiful woman clad in precious little. In fact, he continued his inner dialogue, while his mind carried on its pleasurable games, it would be *unnatural* if the woman sitting next to him didn't evoke a response. He was a red-blooded man of the world merely appreciating what nature had to offer. He was in the middle of reasoning to himself that in fact the desire to feast his eyes on her strikingly tall, voluptuous and entirely womanly body was very similar to a desire to feast his eyes on anything that was aesthetically pleasing, be it a piece of architecture, a stick of furniture or a houseplant in bloom for that matter, when he became aware that she was talking to him.

'What?'

'I asked where we were going to eat.'

'Oh. Just an Italian restaurant I frequent. Five minutes away.' A quick shift of his eyes gathered in brown hands resting languidly on her lap and crossed legs. 'Should make a change from staying in.' He realised when he drew in a shuddering breath that his iron self-control was slipping. 'So tell me about what you do in Panama,' he said, steering the conversation into safe waters that might drown out his wildly soaring thought patterns. 'You never mentioned what you do in the evenings. I don't suppose there's much happening.'

'Depends what you call "not much happening",' Destiny told him. 'If you're asking whether there's much by way of expensive restaurants, clubs and hectic night life, then, no, it's the most boring place on the face of the earth.'

'A simple answer would have been enough.' He pulled sharply into a vacant space that had suddenly become free then turned to face her, one hand lingering on the gear lever between them. 'No need to launch into a biting attack.'

Destiny stared at him for a moment and it occurred to her that she was *never* sarcastic. Now and again, she and Henri would have little ribbing sessions with one another, and they were accustomed to dissecting the magazines that accumulated dust in one of the storage cabins with cutting jokiness, but that was as far as it went. Callum had asked her once before where she had dredged her sarcasm from, but in all truth it was a talent that had only been brought to light with the arrival of the man now sitting next to her, watching her with those cool, disturbing blue eyes.

'I'm sorry,' she apologised.

'Are you?' He didn't give her time to answer, instead twisting round to get out of the car, and she did the same.

'I feel very sorry for whatever man is in your life,' he remarked, holding the door open for her, and she snapped back,

'Funnily enough, I'm only sarcastic when I'm around you.'

'I've had a variety of effects on women in my lifetime,' he murmured into her ear, 'but sarcasm was never one of them.'

Destiny refused to collaborate in his sneering at her expense. Instead, she held her head high and strode ahead of him into the restaurant, for once not feeling overawed by her surroundings.

For starters, she wasn't dressed like someone who had accidentally forgotten the basic rules of fashion.

For another thing, she was so conscious of the man behind her, talking to the head waiter, that she barely noticed her surroundings, never mind how she fitted into them.

She was aware, however, that more than one set of eyes had swivelled in her direction, and she felt a little jolt of pleasure at the minor sensation she had aroused. Even the waiter, as usual a good head shorter than her, was doing his best to hide his interest.

'Your skirt is so damned short—' he leaned across the table as soon as they were seated and looked at her through narrowed eyes '—that even the waiter's staring.'

'It was recommended to me by the sales lady,' Destiny pointed out coolly. '*She* didn't appear to think that it was too short.'

'Well, she should be shot. If you belonged to me, I wouldn't let you leave the house in that get-up.'

He sat back as they were handed two oversized menus, giving her a few seconds for her simmer to reach near boiling point.

'If I *belonged* to you? If I *belonged* to you? People aren't *possessions!*' She stared at him and he gazed back at her, his dark brows meeting in a frown.

'Any woman that was mine would be *my* possession, body and soul.'

'And how would you feel if she felt the same way about you? That she wanted you to dress down because you looked too sexy in what you wear?'

'Are you trying to tell me that you think I'm sexy?'

he asked, turning her well-meaning point on its head and giving her a slow, amused smile.

She muttered something under her breath and resorted to the relative safety of her menu, behind which she could hide. Why ever had she thought that these huge menus were a bit of a joke when in fact they served a very useful purpose as shield from a nerve-jangling dinner companion?

'Well, you still haven't answered my question. Do you?' He pulled down the menu with one finger and peered at her over the top of it, his amused grin much broader now.

'You're an attractive enough man,' she told him—because an outright lie would have probably turned the amused grin into a guffaw of disbelieving laughter. 'If you go for your type of look.'

'*My* type of look?'

He looked neither taken aback nor offended by her postscript. Of course, he *would* she thought irritably. Hadn't she discovered that his ego was roughly the size of Panama? If Stephanie ever sought her advice on the subject, she would tell her in no uncertain terms that scooting around him and never answering back was a sure-fire way to add to the problem.

'I can't read the menu with you dragging it down.'

'Have the fresh fish. It's the best thing on the menu.'

'There you go again,' she reminded him, 'being bossy again,' and blushed when she realised that he had been winding her up.

'So what *is* my type of look?' he persisted, still grinning and still tugging her menu down so that she couldn't conveniently hide behind it.

'Well, if you *must* know, it's that obvious tall, dark-haired, good-looking kind of look.'

'Ah! You mean as opposed to the short, fair-haired, unappealing kind of look…' He released the menu so that her glare of infuriation was lost on the list of starters, and by the time she had decided on what she was going to eat he had his amused gleaming expression safely under wraps.

'I've got all the paperwork here,' he said, whisking a two-inch wad of papers from the briefcase at the side of his chair. He pushed them across to her, then sat back to inspect her at his leisure. 'Naturally you'll need some information on Felt's profit and loss over the past, say, three years. Did you bring it along with you?'

'You know I didn't.' She glanced at the top page and found enough technical terms in the first three sentences to reduce her to bewildered dismay.

'Ah, yes. You were sporting your minimalist look. Not to worry…' He fished into his briefcase again and this time the wad was three inches thick. 'I have everything you need right here.'

'Perhaps you could just sum it all up for me and leave me with this paperwork to read over the next couple of days.'

'You might not understand all the terms and subclauses,' he said piously. 'You might find that I have to explain them to you.'

'I'll try my best to get to grips with it.'

'Okay. Just offering my services to speed things up a bit.' He paused just long enough for them to order their meal, his eyes shooting up at her rejection of his fish suggestion, then leaned forward with his elbows resting on the table. 'If you turn to page fifteen, you'll find a listing of all my company's assets.'

Destiny obligingly turned to the required page and was confronted by columns of figures, none of which appeared to have under six noughts in it. His company, or rather his holdings, were hugely profitable. It didn't take a degree in accountancy to see that.

'Now, if you turn to page eighteen of the document underneath, you can have a quick look at how Felt's been performing recently.'

'Get to the point. I *know* they've been struggling over the past few months.'

'Years, actually.'

'Well, years, then.'

'It's going to require a massive injection of cash to come up to scratch. No amount of good intentions and sympathetic man-management is going to haul it out of the red.'

Destiny was busily surveying the papers in front of her, which seemed to have a huge amount of brackets around figures. She sighed and flicked through the rest of the paperwork. Report upon report, all bearing the ominous word *losses*. Without the optimism of the directors, desperate to hang on to their lucrative jobs, the facts staring her in the face were sinister. She looked up to see Callum staring at her and sipping his wine.

'I can see you're beginning to get the picture.'

'Derek seems to think that there's a chance…'

'Derek's a lawyer who doesn't want me to buy the company,' he said bluntly.

'Why? My uncle had agreed to sell…'

'Because he could see sense.'

'Why should Derek care one way or another?'

'Because his links with that miserable uncle of yours stretch back a long way. Felt's started as a family firm and the family firm was good to him. Unfortunately, it's caused him to develop a very unhealthy blind spot when it comes to common sense.'

Destiny shuffled the papers she was holding and shoved them back to him.

'Why are you so keen to buy something that's losing money hand over fist? No one else wants it, apparently, so why do you?'

'Let's just say that I see it as a worthwhile investment.' He drained the contents of his glass in one long gulp, while his eyes flicked over her face. 'You asked me once whether there was anything personal involved and I might just as well tell you the sordid story of your dear, generous uncle.'

'He was never dear to me,' she said swiftly. 'I never knew him.' She too drained her glass of wine, to ease some of the tension building up inside her.

'You should count your blessings.' He scrutinised her face. The green eyes staring steadily back at him were curious but interested. What was it about this woman? She was a good listener, he thought with a jolt of unease. She must be—or why else would he be feeling this irrational urge to start pouring out details of his private life? And she was compassionate. He felt a sudden, weakening spurt of jealousy at all those countless people who commanded her time out there in the wilds of Panama.

'My father and your uncle knew one another. Once. When they were both young men. Felt Pharmaceuticals began its life as a joint venture between two men who'd graduated from the same university. My father was the brains of the partnership but old Abe had the flair.' The interruption of their food arriving was an irritation that suspended his tale for a few seconds but, now that he had begun, he found that he couldn't stop the tide. She dipped into her food, tucking her sun-bleached hair behind her ears as she ate.

'What happened?' she asked, glancing at him, then back to her food.

'Their little venture took off. They both had money and my father invested everything in the scientific side of the company. Everything seemed hunky dory for a while, then something happened. Or at least that's the story my mother told me years afterwards. Your uncle changed. He became greedy. Greedy and bitter.'

'You mean he had a fallout with your father?'

'None that my mother was ever aware of. He just changed. He became bitter with the world and my father was the first to feel it. He had sunk everything he possessed in building the company, only to find that Abe began working against him, pulling the ground from under his feet. In the end, of course, the politics became too much and the company began to run into financial trouble. Three years after it started, it folded. My father was left with debts he could never hope to repay. He discovered later that some creative accounting had gone on. Abe retreated with a huge amount of cash scattered everywhere, cash that couldn't be touched. He drove my father out of the business and then restarted it under his own name and never looked back. My father spent the rest of his days trying to repay debts that should have been shared. He died a broken man and my mother was left having to raise a child in virtual poverty.' He dug into his food and felt all the old resentment weighing him down like an anchor.

'You mean you've spent your life looking forward to the day when you could get your revenge?'

'When I could get back what was rightfully mine.'

'But all of that…was history. How could it motivate you for so long?'

'I saw it as evening the scales of justice.'

'And now I'm the one you want to hurt? Because of my uncle? How could that be right? I haven't done anything.'

'I don't want to hurt you. But I want the company, which is why I'm prepared to pay over the odds for it.'

'And was Stephanie all part of your revenge?' she asked quietly. 'Did you see her as one more step in making my uncle pay his dues?'

'Don't be ridiculous.'

'How did you meet her?' Having done justice to her enormous plate of food, she closed her knife and fork and rested both elbows on the table, on either side of the plate.

Somehow the conversation had run away, and she was fully in control.

'Why don't we stop concentrating on me and start concentrating on *you*,' he said, pushing his plate away and sitting back into his chair with his fingers resting lightly on the table.

'Because my life isn't as interesting as yours.'

'Oh, please!' He shot her a look of reproving disbelief.

'Well, it's not so full of complications and personal sagas.' Which made his life sound, he thought, as if it had been lifted from a tawdry third-rate soap opera.

'Because of course, everyone is brimming over with love and joy where you live.'

'Because most of us don't have the time to get embroiled in each other's lives.'

'Oh, don't give me that.' Now that she had managed to drag his confession out of him, he could feel himself growing resentful and defensive as he tried to claw back some of his self-assurance. What next? he thought. An outburst of weeping? Some ghastly cleansing of the soul?

'You're saying that all of you meander along in a saintlike fashion, smiling and thinking pure thoughts all the time?' He glared savagely at her and she began to laugh. A maddening laugh which she tried to stifle. Tried and failed.

'No, I'm not saying that at all,' she said seriously, although the corners of her mouth were still twitching with repressed amusement. 'We argue and get frustrated just like the next person.'

'And what about the pure thoughts?' he asked slyly. 'Isn't the heat supposed to up the libido?'

'I wouldn't know,' Destiny said primly, flushing. She thought of Henri and wondered whether her libido had ever been active when she had been around him. They knew each other so well. A deep bond of trust and friendship that was half-cultivated by their circumstances. But *desire? Lust?* She had occasionally fancied that she loved him, and had certainly responded to his flirtation, but the temptation to take things one step further had never been there.

She looked surreptitiously at the man sitting opposite her. All dark, dangerous arrogance. Just the sort of man bemoaned by women's magazines. Well, they certainly didn't tell you how much men like that got under your skin and worked away there until just thinking about them was enough to send your pulses into overdrive, did they?

'Oh, surely you must have had a quick kiss and a grope behind the bushes by the river...'

At any other time she would have told him to mind his own business, but the food and the wine had made her mellow. Even the way he was looking at her, with lazy, brooding interest, sent a little dart of excitement shooting around her body. She was beginning to understand any number of the little games that men and women played, games that had no part on their compound.

'Behind the bushes by the river at night is the last place you would want to be, believe me.' She drank some more wine, which was going down more smoothly and more quickly with each mouthful.

'But it would just instil an element of danger, wouldn't it?' He swirled the liquid in his glass round and round and continued to stare at her with languid blue eyes.

'Snakes? Reptiles? Nasty slippery things that wouldn't hesitate to attach themselves to your ankle if you weren't looking out for them? You're telling me that all that adds up to an exciting element of danger?' She made a face and he smiled slowly at her. Conversation with Henri was never like this. He teased her, but his banter was harmless. This didn't feel harmless. In fact, it felt strangely erotic. She blushed with sudden guilty awareness, and reassured herself that it was all in her imagination. Sophisticated men and women, living in big cities, spoke like this to one another, she decided naively.

'Would you care to see the dessert menu?' The waiter was somehow standing by them. She hadn't even seen him approaching.

'Yes, please.'

'You're going to *have dessert?*' He made it sound as though she had committed an unforgivable crime and her outstretched hand paused.

'Shouldn't I?'

'Of course you should. It's just that the women I've dated in the past have avoided dessert like the plague.'

'Why?' She took the menu and looked at it, trying not to salivate at the descriptions of things done with chocolate and fruits and cream.

'Obsession with their figures,' he said drily.

'I have a big frame,' Destiny said defensively. Come to think of it, she *had* noticed the way Stephanie had refrained from piling food onto her plate. Unlike her. Stephanie had taken minuscule amounts, eaten very slowly and declined seconds. Unlike, come to think of it, her. 'And anyway,' she continued, after having ordered tiramisu with lots of cream, 'I don't get to eat food like this. It's a novelty.' Besides, she told herself, eating less wasn't going to reduce her height, was it? It would just turn her into one of those skinny women she saw in the magazines who seemed to have not much of anything.

'So,' she said, when the tiramisu was in front of her, 'I'm not going to feel guilty about this.'

'You shouldn't. It's very refreshing to meet a woman with a hearty appetite.'

'Would you like some?' She held out the spoon, feeling very relaxed and daring, and he leaned forward. At the very moment that his mouth circled the spoon their eyes met, blue tangling with green, and she felt a rush of blood invade her system, burning like a sudden high fever.

'It's very good.' His eyes never left her face, even after he had sat back and was sipping his cup of coffee. He just continued to stare at her over the rim of the cup.

'I have a proposal for you,' he said slowly. He reached forward before she could say anything and his finger brushed the side of her mouth. 'Cream just there,' he said.

'What kind of proposal?' Just where he had touched felt inflamed. What would it be like to have those fingers travel the length and breadth of her body? She felt another hot wave of guilt wash over her. The man was engaged to her stepcousin! He had done nothing inappropriate, so why was her body disobeying her head and behaving as though he had? She pushed the remainder of the dessert away from her and sternly told herself to buckle down and get her act together.

'First of all, tell me why you're so intent on hanging on to the company. I've told you my dark secret, so what's yours?'

'I don't *have* any dark secrets.' She eyed the near completed two bottles of wine and realised that she'd drunk far more than she had imagined. Oh, blessed relief. The wine was the culprit behind her sordid thoughts! 'The truth is that if I hang on to the company, I can help my father with his research. Derek says—'

'Stop referring to Derek as though he's a guru,' Callum inserted irritably.

'Well, my father's working on a cure for certain tropical illnesses using plant products. You'd be surprised how many cures can come from the trees and the leaves of certain plants. We have routine inoculations for the local people against certain diseases, but they still practise an awful lot of home remedies and the majority of them work, if not all. Felt Pharmaceuticals has the technology to help with further research. If I sell the company to you, I won't have access to their specialised equipment, which would be very useful for my father.'

'So we have the insoluble dilemma.' He signalled to the waiter for the bill and settled it with a platinum credit card, barely looking at it in the process. 'Sell to me and lose that possible source of aid or hang on to the company and go down sinking. You've seen the figures. Either way, you're on a loser. But, as I said, I have a proposal...'

'Which is?'

'Has the guru Derek elaborated on everything you've inherited?'

'Well, I have the details in the house somewhere... So

far, I haven't had much of an opportunity to look at them,' she admitted, 'I've been so wrapped up with the company problems.'

'Well, in addition to the house in London, Abe had a country estate. Some of the contents he willed to his various past dependants…'

'How do you know about that?' Destiny interrupted, frowning and recalling some mention of a place in the country.

'Because Stephanie is one of the heirs. The point is this—the actual manor was willed to you, as were the lands.'

'Manor? Lands?'

'Didn't Derek the guru explain *any* of this to you?' Callum asked incredulously.

'Stop calling him "the guru," and yes, he did mention that there was a house somewhere outside London. I didn't pay much attention. I just assumed that it was, you know, a normal little *house*…' Her voice drifted away as his expression changed from incredulity to amusement.

'You mean, something small and detached with a pristine square of grass around it? A hedge or two, perhaps? Maybe a tree?'

'Something like that,' she agreed.

'How right you were when you said you knew nothing of your dear uncle. Abe was always fond of making sure that everyone knew exactly how wealthy he was. He had a mansion in Berkshire, surrounded by twenty acres of land, quite of bit of it cultivated.'

'Oh, right.'

'I gather you're less than impressed.'

'Why would he want two houses?'

'Lots of people in London enjoy having a bolt-hole in the country,' he explained a little too patiently for her liking. 'Abe just liked having a very *large* bolt-hole. Ready to go?' He stood up and she hurriedly scrambled to her feet, tugging down the dress self-consciously while he watched with an inscrutable expression.

'So here's what I propose. In exchange for Abe's country retreat, I'll work with you. I'll plough as much money into the company as I need to so that it's up and running. Of course, I shall have to take a number of your shares from you, but you'll be the head of the company and entitled to your share of whatever profits it makes— which, with the right management, could be considerable. Your father would also have privileged access, naturally, to whatever medical facilities he needs in our own research centres.'

'Would you say that that's a good deal?' she asked dubiously, trying to work out the pros and cons and failing. At the moment, she felt as though trying to do anything logical with her mind was a bit like trying to build a house of cards in a high wind.

'I'd say you should give it very careful thought,' he told her, as they drove slowly back to her house.

'Why would you want a country house?' she asked.

'Why do you ask so many questions?'

'Because it's the way I am. Oh, I think I understand. Is it so that you have somewhere in the country for you and Stephanie, when you begin to have children?' She would have liked children. Of course, she was only young and had all the time in the world, but time had a nasty habit of slipping away when you weren't looking.

'No, that's *not* the reason,' he was saying impatiently. 'Naturally, you'd have to see the house. I wouldn't want you to consider anything until you're in full possession of all the facts.'

'Naturally.' Sooner than expected, the car was pulling

up to the front of her pristine house. Strangely, the place was beginning to feel a bit like home, even though she still had an instinctive aversion to the English preoccupation with ordered greenery. She slung open her door and preceded him to her front door. It was much cooler now. She unlocked the door, pushed it open and then turned to face him. His face was all angles and his hair was raked back so that there was no relief from the chiselled perfection of his features. He was also standing too close to her. Claustrophobically close.

'Thank you for dinner,' she told him politely, eyes skirting any possible clash with his by focusing on the terraced row of houses visible over his right shoulder. 'Do you want me to take the files with me and have a proper read?'

'So I suggest this weekend. I'll pick you up on Saturday morning and we can return on Sunday night. That should give you long enough to have a look around.'

'Pick me up?' she stammered, confused by this alarmingly swift turn of events. Ever since Derek Wilson had stumbled his way to the compound, her life seemed to have adopted a galloping speed that was quickly turning into a sprint.

'You *do* want to see your country place, don't you? See whether you want my proposal to go ahead?'

'Yes, of course, but…'

'Don't tell me you have plans for the weekend.'

'No, b-but…'

'Then why are you stuttering and acting as though you've been pushed into a corner?'

'It's all a bit sudden, that's all.'

'I'm a great believer in the saying that there's no time like the present.'

That, she thought, was glaringly obvious. But a weekend? Alone with him? It wouldn't do. She couldn't face down what the man did to her and she had no intention of being in his company without remission for days on end. She didn't understand what she was feeling, but she knew that it was all wrong. Mild-mannered Henri with his easy ways and his light-hearted flirting was something she could handle. But Callum unleashed different, frightening things in her. A weekend being frightened was not on her agenda.

'I'd like Stephanie to come,' she said bluntly.

'I intended to ask her along,' he lied. 'I'll see you on Saturday. Around nine.' He looked away, showing her his profile. 'We can all get to know one another a little better.'

CHAPTER FIVE

THE following day, Stephanie asked Destiny to lunch. *A gorgeous little wine bar in Chelsea. You'll adore it.*

What was the dress code, she wondered, for gorgeous little wine bars in Chelsea? The flowered dress which she'd bought on her shopping trip made her feel frivolous. It was added to the list of new emotions which she had been accumulating ever since she'd set foot on British soil. Sometimes she felt as though the perfect bliss she had achieved for all those years in Panama had been an illusion. Back there, she'd operated on one level only. She had been calm, useful, productive and down to earth. Devoting her life to other people had left no room for anything else.

Now, it was as if the small world she had busily and happily occupied had grown and swelled into a complex network of different facets. She no longer felt nauseated and overwhelmed by the crowds. She was becoming accustomed to the buildings that rose around her like the tall, lush trees that encroached upon the compound and to the pace of life that left no time to be alone with the privacy of your thoughts for company. She hadn't read a book since she had arrived! In Panama, she had read voraciously every evening, all manner of books, which she stocked up on in quantity whenever a trip to the city was made and, of course, her father's medical journals, which she had started reading for interest from the age of fourteen.

And men had always been her equals. Aside from

Henri, who had worked alongside her for two years and
whose gallantry rescued her from total asexuality, she'd
had no experience of being aware of them in a sexual
manner. She discussed problems with them, joined in
their conversations, worked with them—but those peculiar antennae that were so finely tuned to their masculinity had never really got going with her. Callum had been
the one to bring that side of her to life. It was a good
thing that she was going to see Stephanie. Her stepcousin
would put a bit of necessary perspective on what was
going on in her head.

Destiny arrived at the wine bar, late but calmly resolved to sort out the problem with Callum and the wayward, puzzling effect he had on her, with the same calm
determination that had always seen her through the
thousands of minor crises that she had faced in her life.
Crises of a more practical nature, but no less surmount-
able than the problem of Callum Ross. Which, anyway,
was an inconvenience but hardly a crisis.

When she cast her mind back to their dinner the night
before, she could feel her heart-rate speed up and that
would never do.

Stephanie was waiting for her at a corner table of the
wine bar. It was obviously a place to go with the fashionable crowd. Rows of men in business suits were
lounging by the circular bar, idly drinking but more interested in who was walking through the door. Some of
them were with women, who were also smartly dressed
in well-tailored suits to match their well-tailored short
haircuts. The tables were all occupied, mostly with
groups of people talking loudly, gesticulating, and laughing.

The décor was very modern. Pale colours, wooden
floor, large abstract paintings on the wall of the kind

painted by some of her eight-year-old children on the compound. Just splashes of paint that looked as though some idiot had spilled his palette on a canvas and hadn't been bothered about cleaning it up.

Stephanie stood up and waved and Destiny scurried over to the table and sat down.

'It's very crowded, isn't it?' She leaned forward and glanced around her, smiling.

Her stepcousin grinned. 'I know. It's brilliant, isn't it? Callum hates crowds like this, but I love it. What's the point making an effort getting dressed if no one's going to be around to appreciate it?' She was in a smoky blue fitted dress, very short, and her nails were painted the exact coral shade of her lipstick. This was Callum's fiancée, Destiny reminded herself, and incidentally everything a man like him would want in a woman. Neat, attractive, vivacious, always smiling, always amenable.

'I wouldn't know,' Destiny admitted, breaking off to order some mineral water and a salad, taking the lead from Stephanie and remembering Callum's reaction at her hearty appetite. 'I can't say that dressing up was something that happened much on the compound. No need.' She grinned. 'And no dressing-up clothes either, come to think of it.'

Which revived all the open-mouthed fascination that Stephanie had shown previously. Whenever she leaned forward her wavy brown hair swung over her shoulders, and she would flick it back by running her fingers through it and then tossing her head the way a horse tossed its mane.

She wanted to know everything about Destiny—her life, her education, what it felt like to live so far away from decent shops, what she ate, what she drank, whether she'd ever had malaria, what the people out there looked like, what her father looked like. When the subject came round to Henri, whose name had been mentioned casually, but had been picked up with the perceptiveness of someone well versed in the ways of relationships, Stephanie shot her a coy smile.

'So there *is* more to life there than you let on!' She giggled. 'What does he look like?'

'You've hardly touched your salad,' Destiny said wryly, dodging the questions she could see hovering on the horizon. Stephanie obligingly stuck a couple of lettuce leaves in her mouth and continued to survey her stepcousin with a gleam in her blue eyes.

'Okay. He's about my height, brownish hair, specs, thinnish.'

'Any more *ishes* to add to the description? What about sexyish?'

No, that describes *your* lover, was the thought that flashed through Destiny's head, disappearing before it had time to take root.

'Yes, well…' she said vaguely.

'I can see—' Stephanie sat back and arched her eyebrows meaningfully '—that you're overwhelmed by lust for this man.'

'It's too hot out there to get lusty.'

'Oh, yeah?'

'Too sticky.'

'Right. In that case, I'm surprised anyone has babies.'

'Tell me about Callum,' Destiny said, going red and rapidly changing the subject, which was greeted with another arch of perfectly bowed eyebrows, but Stephanie grinned and relented.

'What about him?'

'You must be very excited at the thought of getting married…' Her salad had already settled in her stomach and steady hunger pangs were beginning to set in. How could anyone exist on a handful of shrubbery with a bit of black pepper on top?

'Well, we're not *getting married*. Least, not yet.' The heart-shaped face suffused with delicate colour.

'Oh.'

'It's just that the time isn't right,' she rushed on, blushing madly. 'You know...'

'Well, not really, but it's none of my business anyway.'

'Yes, it is! I mean, you're the closest thing I have to a relative. At least, a relative of my own age. I have a couple of aunts in Cornwall but they're in their nineties.' She wrinkled her nose, considering the dilemma of her relativeless state, then her face cleared slightly. 'It's just that...you know...Callum and I... Well, he's pretty busy...work and such...'

'Why don't you tell him to make some time for you?'

Stephanie shrugged and chewed her lip. 'It's not as easy as all that.'

Destiny inclined her head to one side and listened. The waiter efficiently cleared their table, routinely asking whether everything was satisfactory, to which she replied, honestly, 'There wasn't enough of it.'

'I shall tell our head chef,' the man said with an expression that told her that he had no intention of doing any such thing.

'I mean,' Stephanie said in a rush, 'Callum's so *over-powering* and he *hates* women who nag. When we first started going out, he used to say that he loathed women who were demanding.'

'So what?' Destiny frowned, trying to work this out in her head. 'If you don't demand certain things, how on earth do you ever get them?'

Another helpless shrug. 'Thing is, we met at a business do that Uncle Abe had hosted before he and Mum divorced, and he sort of swept me off my feet to start with. You wouldn't believe the women who would love to be seen with him...'

'I can't see why if he's that intolerant.' But she could. He drew stares from other people. He was physically commanding. He had the sort of personality that compelled other people's attention.

'Oh, he's so rich and powerful and awe-inspiring.'

'I don't think he's awe-inspiring. Actually, sometimes he irritates the life out of me.'

'But you'd never let him know that, would you?'

'Yes. Why not? He's not going to chop both my arms off if I say what's on my mind.'

Stephanie looked at her as though she had suddenly discovered that she was dealing with a madwoman.

'Anyway,' Destiny said hastily, 'tell me about this wonderful house I shall be going to see on the weekend. Has Callum told you about his offer?' Which he hadn't, unsurprisingly, so she spent a few minutes telling her stepcousin the details.

'So what will you do?' Stephanie asked, while Destiny wondered why her fiancé had chosen to withhold such important news from the woman he loved. 'If he's made such an offer, then you know he'll expect you to accept. He never compromises when it comes to business.' She giggled nervously. 'Or anything else, for that matter.'

'I don't care *what* he expects. I shall have a look around and come to my own conclusions.' Now, from her stepcousin's expression, she was listening to someone from another planet speaking in forked tongue. Destiny gave a little sigh, plunged into an unrevealing conversation about Henri because she knew that it would distract her stepcousin, and left the restaurant half an hour later wondering what exactly was the nature of the relationship between Stephanie and Callum. Was it any wonder that she had no time to read over here? There was far too much drama in her everyday life to leave much room for a bit of mindless escapism.

Whatever the dress code was for a trip to a country house—*her* country house, as Derek had explained in length on the telephone the day before—Destiny didn't care. She packed comfortable clothes. A spare pair of jeans, two tee-shirts, flat walking boots, a pair of wellingtons. She had worked out that she now possessed roughly twice the amount of clothes she had ever had at any one time before. Aside from when she had been boarding in Mexico.

She managed to cram everything she was taking into her rucksack, and Stephanie's first words on seeing her at ten past nine on the Saturday morning were, 'Is that all you're bringing?'

Destiny slung her bag into the back seat and then folded her long body into the car next to it.

'It's only a weekend,' she pointed out. 'Hello, Callum.' She belatedly addressed the back of his dark head. It seemed that meeting Stephanie for lunch had not managed to put some vital perspective on her wayward feelings because, as their eyes met in the rearview mirror, she could feel her skin tingle.

'My make-up takes up nearly as much room as that,' Stephanie was saying cheerfully. 'Doesn't it, Callum?'

'If not more.' He pulled out of the enclosed cul-de-sac, and reached over to hand her an envelope. 'One or two photos of your little house,' he said drily. 'Thought you might be interested.'

The bundle of twenty-odd photos, rescued from

Stephanie's photo album from the times she had gone
there years previously, before her mother had joined the
line of ex-Felts, showed a sprawling mansion with a series of outbuildings, curling around a swimming pool.
From the front seat, Stephanie craned backwards to explain the photos. The outbuildings had apparently been
used for stabling horses but were now empty and the
swimming pool had been put in at the insistence of her
mother, who had seen it as adequate compensation for
being deprived of living full-time in the city. The grounds
were extensive and included a wood, a stream and or-
chards of fruit trees.

'Who looks after it now?' Destiny asked, still puzzled
by the need her uncle had felt to possess a house of that
size in which people could lose each other without a great
deal of trouble.

'Derek kept on a skeleton staff,' Callum said from the
front. 'He assumed that you'd probably want to sell but,
if you didn't, I suppose he thought that you might want
the retainers to stay. I have no idea how many people
he's kept or what they're doing there for that matter. We
haven't been to the place for months. They could have
hijacked the silver and cleared off for all I know.'

'I thought you said that the contents were willed
to…lots of other people?'

'Certain of the contents, yes. Which would still leave
quite a bit *in situ*.'

'So is there anyone there now?' She had visions of
arriving at an inhospitable mansion, stone-walled and
freezing cold.

'Stephanie got in touch with Harold and his wife to
open up and get the place ready. Or, should I say, get a
small part of the place ready. A lot of the rooms have
never been used.'

'What a waste.'

She noticed that they were now leaving London and was heartened by the sight of greenery. It must be easy to forget the existence of open land when you were constantly surrounded by buildings.

'What would you do with the house if...I decided to go ahead with your proposal?'

'Convert it into something, I expect.'

'Convert it into what?'

'A hotel.'

'You'd convert this beautiful old mansion into a *hotel*?'

'I would convert a beautiful old mansion into a *beautiful old hotel*,' he said, with a trace of impatience in his voice. 'At least it would be used. What difference would it make to you, anyway? Do you intend staying in England?'

'No, of course not.'

'This is all premature speculation anyway. Let's just get to the damned place and see how you feel about it then.' He accelerated as they cleared the outskirts of London and hit the motorway, and Destiny lapsed into silence, watching the scenery flash by. Summer was still holding its own and the blue, cloudless skies made everything seem crisp and fresh.

They were at the village before eleven, and Stephanie, who appeared to have drifted off into a light sleep, was revived at the sight of a few shops and the prospect of getting out of the car and stretching her legs. She launched into an animated conversation about what she'd used to do when she went to stay at the country manor, interrupting herself frequently to remark on the dullness of country life.

'It must be an awful lot more peaceful than living in

London, though,' Destiny pointed out, liking the feeling of space and calm around her. The small village, with its pubs and little stone shops and parish church, had none of the threatening claustrophobia of London. And the air was much fresher. She had rolled down her window, ignoring Callum's comment about the air conditioning in the car, and closed her eyes briefly, enjoying the breeze through the window.

'Stephanie isn't enamoured of peace,' he said drily, speaking about her as though she wasn't sitting next to him—and, in all fairness, Stephanie didn't object.

'And are you?' Destiny asked, looking around her now with interest as the car slowed on the narrow lane and turned left up an avenue lined with trees. Ahead of them, a pair of massive wrought-iron gates were open, and beyond them lay fields and pastures. 'Or do you prefer living in the fast lane, where you can stride around, giving orders to everyone and enjoying having the world bow down to you?'

Stephanie uttered an incoherent squeak of horror and looked around at Destiny, who grinned airily back at her.

'Sorry,' she said politely. 'I shouldn't have said that.'

'Sorry? You? For having said something you shouldn't? Why? Why break habits of a lifetime?' But there was lazy amusement in his voice. 'These are all part of the grounds. The sheep keep the grass down, but there are still six acres of lawned land. Look ahead. You can see the house coming into view.'

She leaned forward and watched as the impressive façade rose up ahead of them, like a matriarch surveying her domain. She had never seen anything quite like it before in her life. The fact that it belonged to her seemed unreal.

'Did you bring a swimsuit?' Stephanie asked suddenly.

'It's hot enough for us to swim and I could do with a tan. I can't bear English weather. All rain and fog and light drizzles.'

'I don't possess a swimsuit,' Destiny told her.

'Not at all?' Her stepcousin sounded horrified.

'No.'

'But how are you going to go into the pool? I'm sure I have a couple here, but you'd never fit into them!'

'I shall have quite enough to do looking around, honestly.' The thought of trying to cram her huge frame into one of her stepcousin's swimsuits wasn't worth thinking about. She looked comical enough next to her as things stood.

In fact, as they all trooped into the overwhelming hall, she wondered whether two days was going to be long enough to see everything. Harold, a wizened middle-aged man with eyes that seemed permanently focused on his feet, welcomed them in and he and Callum conferred in hushed voices for a few minutes, while Destiny continued to stare open-mouthed around her. Stephanie, well accustomed to all the grandeur, stood unimpressed to one side and then, as soon as Harold had disappeared with the cases, announced that she wanted to go for a dip in the pool. *Just in case it decides to rain later. You know what the weather's like over here.*

'Sure you won't come with me and try on one of my swimsuits?' she asked kindly, and Destiny shook her head with a laugh.

'I don't think that would work, do you?' She wanted to tell her stepcousin to run along and have a good time. Even though they were more or less the same age, Destiny felt decades older. There was something very young and childlike about Stephanie, something very much in need of protection. Which brought her round to Callum.

He was standing, watching them with some amusement; and as soon as Stephanie had disappeared up the stairs, lightly running, he turned to her and said in a drawling voice, 'It's hard to believe that you two are roughly the same age. You treat her as though she was your daughter.'

Destiny smiled indulgently. 'Actually, sometimes I feel as though she is. She's so…*young*…in her ways.' She sighed and caught herself. 'Anyway, the house. Should we start now? Looking around? Or do you need time to recover from the car drive? Oh. You may want to go and have a dip in the pool as well,' she added awkwardly. 'I didn't think.'

'No. Playing at being a sun lizard isn't my cup of tea.' He looked at her with a shuttered expression and realised, with a certain amount of confused irritation, that he would have been more than happy to play the sun lizard game if it involved watching her frolic around in a swimming pool with next to nothing on.

He would, he decided, have to speak to Stephanie. Whether he liked it or not, the doubts that had been swelling over the past few months about their relationship were rapidly crystallising into the unpleasantly concrete fact that their relationship was sagging. Sex, which had been satisfactory enough to start with, had been almost nonexistent for months now, and lately had disappeared altogether from the agenda. He could kid himself that his work left him exhausted, but who was he trying to fool? The blunt truth of the matter was that however fond he was of his fiancée, he no longer felt any sexual urges when he was around her.

Why else was he mentally stripping the woman in front

of him now? Wondering what that body of hers would look like uncovered? She was not his type. Too big, too forthright, too damned argumentative and clever. But she was on his mind more than he cared to think. Daydreaming and fantasising about her was obviously a symptom of the malaise in his own personal life.

Realising that he was staring at her, he frowned assertively and said in a clipped voice, 'Right. The house. We'll start with the top and work our way down.'

Destiny vaguely wondered whether two days was going to be enough to complete this daunting task, but she obediently followed him towards the impressive staircase that coiled upwards like a snake. Halfway up, Stephanie came bouncing towards them, towel in hand and a broad smile on her face.

'Off to begin the tour?' she said, pretending to yawn. 'Sitting around the pool would be much more fun,' she said to them.

'Maybe later,' Destiny said, in the sort of placatory voice she used with her children on the compound whenever they asked for something that was patently out of the question. It was the age-old delaying tactic of saying *in a minute,* when a child asked for another glass of juice. And as with a child, it worked, because Stephanie shrugged and grinned and disappeared with a cheerful, *Well, see you both later then* over her shoulder.

What on earth did Callum see in Stephanie? The enigma was enough to bring home to her just how lacking in experience she was. Oh, very experienced when it came to using her brains, and very mature in tackling the day-to-day rigours of living in a jungle, but as green as God's grass when it came to the emotional side of her life.

For goodness's sake, she was still a virgin! She and

Henri had indulged in some light-hearted fondling, but she, for one, had never felt any urge to carry the fondling through to its natural conclusion. Maybe *he* had. Or maybe, she thought, he, like Callum, was really only interested in women who acted like women and not women who were as independent as they were themselves. It was a depressing conclusion. She would never be harbouring these thoughts, she knew, if she hadn't come to this country, and she glared resentfully at the broad, masculine figure ascending the staircase ahead of her because, like it or not, he was the source of her confusion.

Right now, he was giving her a potted history of the house while she continued to scowl safely from behind. Only when they were at the top of the house did she manoeuvre her features into some semblance of politeness, even though she was too aware of him to find the task easy.

'I hope,' he said, turning to her, hands thrust into his pockets, head slightly cocked to one side, 'that I'm not giving you a load of information that you're already aware of.'

'How on earth would I know anything about the history of British architecture?' Destiny snapped edgily.

'You seem to know just about everything else. You speak more languages that any woman I've ever met; you practise medicine; you teach; you single-handedly fight off marauding tigers and crocodiles that have wandered from your river in search of some human dinner.'

'It's not my fault you don't meet the right women,' she retorted sarcastically, instantly regretting her outburst, which wasn't fair because it stemmed from her own sudden lack of self-confidence in her femininity.

'What are you trying to say? That Stephanie is the wrong woman for me?'

'No,' she mumbled, wishing, yet again, that she had controlled her feelings instead of letting him push her into another uncharacteristic response. 'It's very interesting finding out about the house. It's just that knowing about baroque developments in architecture during the Stuart Period isn't exactly handy when you're living in the wilds of Panama. Unless,' she added with a weak stab of humour, 'I intend puzzling those marauding crocodiles into submission.'

He smiled at her, very, very slowly, and she felt as though she had been touched because his smile was so like a physical caress. Her breathing thickened and she looked away quickly. Stephanie was sunbathing downstairs, and wanting to touch this man in front of her was so shocking and so inappropriate that it took her breath away.

For the next couple of hours she meekly followed him from room to room and tried to pretend that he was no more than a tour guide. It helped if she imagined him as a short, fat, bald tour guide.

She didn't glance once at him, which wasn't difficult because there was enough to see in the myriad rooms. From one of them she looked out, and down below she could see the diminutive figure of her stepcousin languidly lying on a poolside deckchair, eyes closed and arms resting over the sides of the chair.

Callum came to stand next to her and immediately the hairs on her arms stood on end.

'What sort of woman do you think would be right for me, then?' he murmured, without looking at her.

During his brisk, factual tour, she had managed to keep everything nicely under control, but now she felt every nerve and pulse in her body stirring and making her feel hot and uncomfortable.

'I think Stephanie's a lovely person.'

'That's not what I asked.'

'You're engaged to my stepcousin. Of course she's the right woman for you.' She didn't dare look at him, but she could feel that he had turned to her and was looking at *her*, and she folded her arms. Her fingernails pressed into her skin.

'You don't believe that. You know you don't.'

'Why are you asking me these questions?' she flung at him, spinning to face him. 'Why does it matter what I think?'

'I'm interested, that's all. I'm not a fool. I've noticed the way you look at us when we're in the same room, seen the expression on your face—as though you're mystified at what I see in her.'

Oh, good Lord. Had she been *that* transparent?

'Maybe you're right,' he said softly, so softly that she wanted to groan. Her body was responding to his nearness, to the low, velvety tone of his voice, to the depths of his eyes resting on her, the way it would have responded if she was standing next to an open fire. An open fire that was slowly but steadily melting her.

The wetness she felt between her legs was such an unknown experience that at first she wasn't even aware of it and, when she was, she was horrified.

This was lust. It bore no resemblance whatsoever to the affection and the tenderness and the light-hearted, detached curiosity she had felt when Henri had occasionally kissed her on the mouth, after a bit of alcohol and under the embrace of a hot starry night. This was like being hit by a sledgehammer.

'Who knows? Do you think I might need a more challenging type of woman?'

'*I* don't know what you need,' she squeaked.

'True. Really, how do any of us know what we need unless we try it out first? Test the water, so to speak?' Then he did something so unexpected and so shocking that for a few seconds her body froze. He touched her. Just with one finger, on her mouth, tracing it, but the touch was so erotic that the ache between her legs shot through the rest of her body like a fast-moving virus. Her breasts actually seemed to hurt and she could feel the pupils in her eyes dilate.

'No!' She pulled back, shaking, and spun round on her heels, staring down at her feet and breathing heavily, while he lounged against the window sill. 'Please,' she whispered, still staring at her feet, 'let's just see the rest of the house. Please.'

Callum didn't answer immediately. He couldn't. He was too busy trying to get his vocal cords into gear. Eventually, more in an attempt to repress the powerful and bloody primal urge he had felt for her than anything else, he said, 'Sure. And if I manage to make it boring enough, who knows? You might just find it useful in boring unwanted animals to death.'

You could never be boring, she wanted to say, but she didn't. He had touched her mouth with his finger and he now felt sorry for her because he must be able to see how inordinately she'd responded. Like the gauche, un-sophisticated primitive that she was. He felt sorry for her and was now trying to put her out of her misery by re-storing some light-hearted humour between them. For that she felt both grateful and mortified at the same time.

But things got easier, and after another hour exploring each room, discussing who'd removed what in accor-dance to the legacy Abe had left, the brief moment of madness, if not forgotten, had been put to sleep. Like a tiger injected with a temporary sedative. She had no doubt that, when she was alone again, the moment would come rushing out at her, like a bat out of hell.

They only managed to cover part of the house, which, if anything, was bigger than it had appeared from the outside, before Callum suggested lunch, and they joined a lazy and slightly browner Stephanie by the pool.

More salad. Destiny looked at her plate, which had been brought out by Deirdre, Harold's other half, with a distinct lack of enthusiasm. At least this time round there was plenty of it, but several helpings went virtually no-where to filling the gap in her stomach.

'Don't worry,' Callum confided, as they left Stephanie once more by the pool and resumed their tour of the house, 'dinner will be more substantial. It's an old English custom to serve salads on hot summer days.'

'Don't know why,' Destiny said. 'You need a lot of energy in hot weather, especially at lunchtime, and the last thing you get from a bundle of lettuce leaves is an injection of energy.'

An injection of apathy, more like it, she thought when they had finally completed the rounds of the house. In the end they had had to quicken their pace, if the gardens were to be done the following day, but there was lots she wanted to revisit.

At six o'clock, when they found themselves once again at the pool, Stephanie was finally through with her day's exertions.

'You look great,' Destiny said warmly. 'Very brown.'

'Do I?' She contorted her slender body in an attempt to scrutinise as much of it as she could. 'What do you think, Callum?'

'Mmm.' He wasn't looking at her, even though his thoughts were most definitely on her. On her and on the chat they would have to have before the evening was over. He hoped to God that she wouldn't break down on him but, if she did, then whose fault was it? His. His, because he should have ended this relationship a long time ago and not relied on fondness to see them through. He could have kicked himself.

'I think that means *yes*,' Destiny offered lightly.

'And how would you know what I mean?' His voice was cold. They both turned to him with varying expressions of surprise and discomfiture, but it was Stephanie who, amazingly, exploded.

'Why do you have to be so rude? Why can't you just *relax* a little and stop acting as though everyone has to do as you say? You…you…you…' Her brief outburst of valiance tapered off while Destiny groaned inwardly and wondered miserably whether her casual words of advice had been taken to heart. She was now a spectator at a scene in which two opponents faced one another, one with an expression of shock but defiance, the other with grim determination.

'I think, Destiny,' Callum said, looking at his fiancée, 'that it's time you relaxed before dinner. Deirdre is in the kitchen. She'll show you up to your room.'

CHAPTER SIX

WHEN Destiny emerged two hours later, she found Stephanie by herself in the kitchen. The table was set, but for two and Stephanie was busily fussing around the stove with a pair of oven gloves on her hands. She'd pulled her hair back into a high ponytail and was wearing a pair of culottes and a silk blouse.

'Callum's gone,' she said, answering the question that hadn't yet been asked.

'Gone where?'

'Back to London. And I told Harold and Deirdre that there was no need for them to stay and see about dinner for the two of us.'

'So you cooked all of this yourself?' She couldn't help it, but there was incredulity in her voice because the smells emanating from the various dishes were mouth-watering and she had somehow never imagined her step-cousin to be much of a hand when it came to culinary skills.

'Lord, no.' Stephanie looked at her and grinned. 'Are you crazy? Toast and scrambled egg are about the only two things I can manage. No, Deirdre cooked all this up herself and gave me very strict instructions on how long I was supposed to heat everything for. She seemed to think that I would wreck her meal.'

'And you haven't.'

'Well, the soufflé *is* in the bin, actually. Forgot it in the oven, and by the time I remembered it was a sad, deflated black mass.' She brought various dishes to the

101

table, filled their glasses with wine and sat down with a little sigh. 'There's enough food to feed an army here. Hope you're hungry because I've lost my appetite.'

'There was no need for you to rise to my defence back then, Stephanie,' Destiny said awkwardly. 'I'm very sorry if…you know… I mean, I wouldn't like to think that you got yourself into trouble because of me…' She looked at the little figure, ridiculously fragile without her usual make-up and with her hair pulled back, toying with the birdlike proportions of food on her plate.

'Don't be silly. It's not your fault.' Stephanie picked up a few vegetables on her fork and proceeded to survey them without much interest. Then she rested her fork on her plate and gulped back some of her wine instead. 'We really should have called it a day a long time ago, but things have a habit of drifting on. On and on and on. We never really argued, but then we never really *spoke* either. We've just been trundling along for the past few months. No excitement, no magic—just two people who got on reasonably well and saw no reason to have any kind of confrontation.'

Until I came along, was the thought that guiltily occurred to Destiny as she tucked into her food. The spread on the table more than compensated for the lunchtime offering of leaves and cold meats, and it was traditional food. Her meals out thus far, in restaurants, had been small, prettily presented plates of various things drizzled with strange juices and accompanied by delicate titbits of vegetables arranged in appetising but unsatisfactory designs. This was hearty food and manna to a ravenous appetite.

'So it's all over?'

'I gave him back his ring and, to be honest, I was pretty relieved. It was all very civilised, actually. More of a discussion than any kind of argument. Callum hates scenes. You could say that we parted the best of friends.'

'Well, that's something at least.'

'I mean, of course I'll miss him. We kind of got accustomed to one another. But that's not enough, is it? Just liking someone and being *kind of accustomed to them?* What kind of marriage would *that* have been? Without any spark at all?'

'I suppose so.' Destiny thought about Henri—not that marriage had ever been on the agenda, although Henri had jokingly suggested it a couple of times.

'I would have ended up being married to someone who could have been my brother!' Some of the liveliness resurfaced and Stephanie managed to eat a couple of mouthfuls of food before closing her knife and fork. 'I realised that what I wanted was thunder and lightning and fireworks, not just feeling good because I was out with someone most women would give their eye teeth to be seen with. Anyway, I also realised that Callum's always treated me like a child. I think he thought that if he spoke to me in more than two-syllable sentences, I might not understand what he was saying!'

'And did you tell him all of this?'

'What would have been the point? It's not like I felt any urge to fight to hang on. I was relieved that we were going to be parting company. Sad but relieved.' She finished her glass of wine and refilled it. 'So now here I am, back on the market, in search of true love.' She tried to look dramatic and mournful but the effect was ruined by tell tale giggles.

'You'll find a partner in less time than it would take me to kill a snake,' Destiny told her, finally closing her knife and fork with a warm, replete feeling in her stomach. 'Think about me and my problems of finding true love! Out in the middle of nowhere! I shall end up a grey, sad little soul—or should I say big soul?—devoting my life to other people while no one devotes their life to me.'

'You have Henri.'

'You remembered his name?'

'I have a very retentive memory when it comes to certain things.'

'Henri…' Destiny stood up and began clearing the table while Stephanie began washing up. 'Henri is… Well, more of a friend…'

'With or without the spark?'

'We get along so well…'

'You're avoiding the question.'

'He's a lovely person. Kind, thoughtful but not boring or fuddy-duddy.'

'Have you slept with him?'

'Stephanie!' She was frankly shocked by the question. Confidences of that nature belonged to a language she had never spoken.

'Well, have you?' Stephanie persisted.

'I…well… You have to understand…'

'You haven't.'

'Well, no…' Destiny's face was bright red and she made a big production of wiping the kitchen table to try and hid the fact.

'And have you been tempted to?'

'It's awfully difficult on a compound, Steph. It's very comfortable, and we all have our own living quarters, but still…'

'Enough said. I'm beginning to get the message!' And they looked at one another with an instant of perfect comprehension. As if by unspoken but mutual consent, they spent the remainder of the evening chatting about everything under the sun apart from Henri and Callum, and when at ten-thirty Stephanie finally uncurled herself from her chair to head to bed, Destiny thought with a pang that she would miss her stepcousin. Miss the frivolity and gossip and giggling that she never got on the compound. She would miss someone taking an interest in what she wore and how she did her hair and offering advice on colour schemes. She would miss the girlish chat about men and their ways and the cosy, secret bond that seemed to exist between women which was a whole great world away from the one in which she had spent most of her life. For the first time she thought of her compound in Panama with a certain amount of detachment, and realised that she had needs that could never really be fulfilled there.

'I'll stay down here for a while longer,' Destiny said, walking with her stepcousin to the door, and was surprised when she received a hug and a broad smile.

'I'm so glad you're here,' Stephanie said to her. 'You're a darling.'

'Well. Thank you.'

'And don't be late up. A girl needs her beauty sleep.'

Her mother had used to tell her that when she had been alive and the cliché brought tears of nostalgia to her eyes.

Destiny settled into a comfortably maudlin mood, aided and abetted by the glass of port which Stephanie had produced with a flourish and insisted that she drink, and was sitting in the smallest of the sitting rooms when she became aware of the sound of footsteps.

If Stephanie was returning for some more words of comfort, then Destiny had no objection. Comforting people was something she did well. She had enough experience of it, comforting mothers with sick children and the occasional new recruit to the compound pining for what they had left behind.

She looked expectantly at the door and blanched when she saw who her visitor was.

'I thought you'd gone back to London.' She had half stood in shock, but now subsided back into her chair, still cradling her glass of port. The drowsy inertia induced by lots of food and the alcohol disappeared at the speed of light and was replaced by a jumpy edginess that made her breathing jerky and painful and dried out her mouth.

'Forgot something,' he informed her, prowling into the room and circling her chair before sitting down on the sofa and stretching his long legs out in front of him. 'What are you drinking?'

'Port.'

'First wine? Now port? Not getting used to the finer things in life, by any chance, are you?' There was an antagonistic edge to his drawl and it occurred to her that he was looking for a fight. And why not? He had probably got halfway to London, more than enough time to think about what had happened between himself and Stephanie. More than enough time to work out that his fiancée's sudden and uncharacteristic behaviour had only seen the light of day since she, Destiny, had been on the scene. Stephanie might well be relieved that it was all over and, who knew, maybe she had really believed that the feeling had been mutual, but it was evident that Callum was far from a happy man. In fact, he was in a foul mood.

'What did you forget?'

'Oh, I forgot that I was supposed to spend tomorrow showing you around all these extensive acres of land.' He made a sweeping, lazy gesture with his hand while he continued to look at her from under his lashes.

'I think I would have been capable of showing myself around.'

'And leave you with the impression that I'm anything less than the perfect gentleman?' He gave a short, harsh laugh and her jumpy nerves became even more jumpy. 'Now, why don't you go and get me a glass of port? It's been one helluva night, as I'm sure you know.'

'The bottle of port is in the kitchen, and if you want me to feel sorry for you then you're not going the right way about it.'

'Why should you feel sorry for me? No, don't answer that one. Not until,' he said, getting to his feet and heading for the door, 'I have a glass of port in my hand.'

Instead of savouring the few minutes he was gone to try and relax, Destiny found that her nerves were stretched to breaking point by the time he came back with a glass in one hand and the bottle in the other.

'So,' he said, resuming his position of indolence on the chair, 'you were saying...'

'I'm sorry that things didn't work out between you and Stephanie,' she said evenly.

'Are you? Why?'

'It wasn't my fault,' she mumbled defensively, allowing her guilty thoughts to surface.

'I never said that it was.' *But it damn well was,* he thought savagely. She'd moved into his complacent life, which had been running quite smoothly, and blown the whole thing to smithereens. Yes, he'd had misgivings about Stephanie, and, yes, he would have ended the whole thing—which, he'd been relieved to discover, had been met with similar feelings of relief. But he would not now be sitting with a drink in one hand with his well-oiled life in pieces around his ankles.

He'd left the house intent on making it back to

London, but in fact had made it only to the nearest pub, where he had drunk far too much for his own good. It was just as well that the pub in question had only been twenty minutes' drive away and there had been a taxi to get him back to the estate.

It was all right and dandy for her to sit there with those bewitching green eyes and look at him as if he was a madman, but she turned him into one. He'd closed the door on one woman, a long overdue closure, and in the process another door had blown open and he had realised, with the sadistic help of a few glasses of whisky, that what he had considered a harmless enjoyment of this woman's conversation had somehow turned into an addiction. He was falling in love with her, and the mere fact that he'd admitted as much to himself was enough to make him realise that he'd probably gone past the point of no return.

He was not only invigorated by her but she had lodged in his soul and he wanted her out. He wanted his control back. He didn't want to sit at his desk with a stack of files in front of him while his mind played games and sabotaged his every effort to work. To work, to sleep, to think clearly.

The woman who had originally been a temporary thorn in his long-range forecast was now driving him crazy.

'Perhaps you two weren't suited to one another,' she was now saying quietly. 'Perhaps the thunder and lightning and fireworks had gone out of the relationship—and what would have been the point of marriage then?' Anyone would think that she, Destiny Felt, the woman with no emotional past to speak of when it came to the opposite sex, was an expert on the subject.

'And what makes you think that thunder and lightning and fireworks are all that necessary to a good marriage?'

he jeered, calling a halt to the alcohol and resting his glass next to him on the ground. 'In case it's missed you, thunder and lightning and fireworks are all over in the wink of an eye.'

'If you want to try and persuade Stephanie to stay with you, then you're talking to the wrong person,' Destiny said cautiously, and he leaned forward and rested his elbows on his knees.

'You mean you won't go upstairs and try and persuade her that my heart is breaking? That I can't go on?'

Destiny tried to imagine this big, muscular man, made of steel, with a breaking heart, and she realised that it hurt to think that Stephanie might be the one to do that.

'Just as well I don't want you to do any such thing, then, isn't it?' He shot her a ferocious, brooding look. 'Because you're right. Steph and I should have reverted into being just good friends a long time ago.' He got up and began his restless prowling around the room while she watched, mesmerised by the way his body moved. For someone of his size, there was a feline grace about him that she wouldn't have expected.

'Of course,' he said, briefly turning to look at her from across the room, 'it hasn't helped that you've instigated the revolution by telling her that she was a poor, downtrodden female who needed to get in touch with herself and start making a stand for women's rights.'

'I did no such thing!' Destiny protested uncomfortably.

'Well—' he shrugged '—she's been quoting you from dawn till dusk. Oh, *Destiny this,* and *Destiny that* and *Destiny the other.'*

'That's not fair,' Destiny said hesitantly, wondering what exactly these quotes were.

'No, it's not, is it?' he countered, strolling over to where she was sitting and looming over her like an avenging angel. 'Because, stuck out in the middle of no-where, you haven't exactly got the experience to be a guru on all things sexual, have you?'

'I never claimed I was!' Destiny said, rising to the occasion. It took a mammoth effort to stare him down, and in all events she didn't manage it, finally lowering her eyes to his knees, which were altogether less alarming than other, less innocent, parts of him.

'Do you know—' he dropped his voice, which was even more alarming than when it was directed at her with all its implicit menace '—that for someone with little or no experience, you do a pretty damned good job of being a siren?'

'Me? A siren?' She laughed, but what emerged was more along the lines of a hysterical choke. 'You're jok-ing, aren't you? Where do you think I've learnt these amazing skills of being a siren? Do you think I practise daily in front of the howler monkeys in the jungle?' She laughed derisively, thinking of her sheltered, protected background which had left all these loopholes she was now falling headlong into.

'You,' he accused, walking towards her so that she coiled back into the chair. He reached out and dropped his hands to either side. 'So philosophical when it comes to giving advice. I bet you and Steph had a good old heart-to-heart while I wasn't here, while I was in that pub burying myself in a few draughts of whisky, man's most reliable friend...'

'I thought you said you were on your way to London...?'

'I was. But the journey ended prematurely at the vil-lage pub. Funny how these things happen.'

They happen, Destiny thought, because—whether you admit it or not—the break-up was traumatic for you. A

man like him would need a submissive woman, a woman
who was willing to bend like a sapling to his powerful
personality, and the minute that Stephanie began showing
signs of rebellion he had reacted with his typical overwhelming intensity. Perhaps the truth of the story was
that Stephanie had ended their relationship and pride
would not let him try to win her back, so, in her relief,
Stephanie had misread his signals for feelings of shared
relief that it was over. It all seemed so horrendously con-
voluted, but wasn't Destiny fast discovering that nothing
here was what it seemed? People dressed, spoke and behaved in a manner designed to create a certain type of
impression, and honesty was something that remained
locked away for a rainy day.

'So you've been drinking,' she accused coolly, and he
gave a bark of humourless laughter.

'A glass or two of whisky. Is that allowed under the
circumstances?'

'You probably need to go to bed,' Destiny said. Her
body was beginning to ache from the unnatural angle in
which she was sitting, pressed back against the chair in
an attempt to ward off the sheer force of his masculinity.

'Is that an offer?'

'No, it's not!' But the suggestion stirred something in
her that sent her already accelerated heart into overdrive.
Bed? With Callum Ross? Naked bodies coated in perspiration, writhing in passion on rumpled sheets. The image was strong enough to almost make her squeak with
terror. 'Look, why don't I make you some coffee?' In
other words, Please let me get out of here and away from
you so that I can pull myself together.

'You think that's what I need?'

'It might…sober you up…'

'I'm not drunk.'

'No, maybe not, but...'

'Oh, why not?' He pushed himself back and stood up, fists balled in his pockets, watching her.

'Black?'

'Whatever.' He shrugged and she escaped out of the room, and, after a moment of brief orientation in the hall to make sure that she headed in the right direction and didn't amble off to some remote corner of the house by mistake, made for the kitchen.

She didn't hear him enter. In fact, she was only aware of his presence when she turned around with the cup of coffee in her hand to find him standing there behind her. In her shock she took two steps backwards, bumping into the counter, and there was a second's delay between the coffee spilling and the sudden burning pain on her hand, where most of it had gone. This time her yelp had nothing to do with him but with her hand.

She dashed the cup on the counter and half ran to the sink, pushing the plug in and filling it with cold water; then she plunged her hand in, gritting her teeth.

'This is your fault!' she wailed. 'If you hadn't sneaked up on me like that, none of this would have happened.' Through the water she could see the raised red smudge where the coffee had touched. It would come up in a nasty blister and hurt for a bit, but it wasn't serious. When she looked at him, though, his face was deathly pale.

'I'm sorry,' he said roughly. 'Do you need to see a doctor?'

'Don't be ridiculous. It's a burn, not a broken hand.'

'God. Abe must have had some kind of first-aid supplies in this bloody mausoleum.' He began pulling open cupboard doors which were either empty, or else yielded stores of pristine, unused china.

'I'll be fine.'

He swung back to her, raking his hand through his hair. 'There's no need to play the martyr, Destiny.'

'I'm not playing the martyr. Look, why don't you go and sit down? Or make yourself another cup of coffee.'

'You're right. It *was* my fault.' He stood next to her and they both watched her splayed fingers under the water. 'How does it feel now? Is that helping? Should I get a dishcloth and soak it in some water? I've got a first-aid kit in my car. No, forget that, the car's at the pub. We can't even get out of this damned place to get you to a hospital!' he groaned, and Destiny sighed deeply.

'It's a coffee burn, for heaven's sake. Surely you must have dealt with this type of thing before?'

'Not really, no.'

'You've never burnt yourself before?'

'Not that I can remember. My mother always taught me to be careful around hot things.' His anger had dissipated, which was good, she thought, although the humour creeping into his voice was almost as dangerous.

She whipped her hand out of the water and said, in a soothing voice, 'There, it feels much better now.'

'Wait there.' He fetched a dry cloth and gently dabbed the water off, while her heart seemed to do a funny kind of somersault and end up somewhere in her throat. 'You'd better come and sit down.'

'You're overreacting!' Destiny protested fruitlessly, as he led her very slowly back into the sitting room, holding her wrapped hand as though it was made of breakable crystal.

'Now, sit.'

She obediently sat on the sofa and, alarmingly, he sat next to her, so that the sofa depressed under his weight and her body slid an infinitesimal amount closer to his, so that they were lightly touching. He gently rested her hand on his leg and removed the cloth.

'Looks much better,' she said weakly.

'Looks bloody awful.'

'You need to feast your eyes on something truly awful, and you'd agree with me that the hand looks fine.'

'Something…like what?'

'Something…like a human missing a bit because of an overhungry croc? Or something…like a person with a hand infected with snake toxin.'

'I don't know how you do it.' Her hand was still on his leg and she looked at him, her mouth half-open, acutely conscious of the feel of his hard thigh under her fingers, even though he seemed blissfully unaware of it.

'Do what?' she asked, shutting her mouth.

'Live the life that you do.' Their eyes met. To her, they seemed to fuse and she felt a wave of giddiness steal over her.

'You make it sound as though I'm some kind of latter-day heroine,' she said a little breathlessly, 'and I'm not.'

'Do you ever long for escape?'

'Don't we all?' She wished that the lighting wasn't quite so dim, but there was no overhead light. The room was lit by a series of lamps, only two of which were actually turned on.

'How's the hand?'

'Barely feel a thing,' she answered truthfully. She dutifully stared at it, and he lightly traced a pattern along her fingers.

'Will you miss this evil city of ours, then? Or are you itching to get back to your country? God, I make it sound as if you're not English, but of course you are. In fact, you even speak better English than most people over here do.'

She laughed nervously. Her hand had developed a will of its own and was enjoying itself on his thigh. 'That's only because my parents were so adamant about speaking it at home. I never really picked up an accent or slang from anyone else. Can you imagine if you spoke English only to your parents?'

'Oh, I can imagine a lot of things—' he paused '—but not that. You still haven't answered me. *Are* you itching to get back to Panama?'

'Is this your way of asking me whether I've made my mind up about the house as yet?' She withdrew her hand from its compromising position and cradled it on her own lap with her other hand.

'No, it's not!' he shot back at her. 'Damn the house. It's the last thing on my mind at the moment.'

Destiny looked at him warily. 'And what is the *first* thing on your mind?'

For a few seconds he didn't answer. He just looked at her until she could feel every drop of colour leave her face and then rush back in a tidal wave, turning her crimson.

'This is,' he muttered. He put his hand at the back of her neck and pulled her towards him, then his mouth met hers.

Or, rather, his mouth assaulted hers. His lips were hungry and his tongue pushed into the moistness of her mouth. His hand pulled her towards him, fingers buried in her thick hair and, after a split second of confusion, during which she made a feeble attempt to break away, Destiny surrendered to all the powerful, primal feelings suddenly released inside her.

From her near-frozen state of virginal innocence, this awakening was explosive. Had she been conducting her entire life in a state of slumber? she wondered. She coiled her arms around his neck, moaning in surprise and pleasure when his mouth left hers to trail wetly along the slim column of her neck.

She knew all about the birds and the bees. Before her mother had died, she had sat Destiny down and told her. And, of course, she had studied enough medical journals to be fully acquainted with the act of mating and reproduction. But what she was experiencing now bore no resemblance to all those clinical explanations she had read about in her youth, and it bore even less resemblance to what she had felt with Henri, during their occasional amateurish gropings.

A wild animal had taken over her body. She writhed and groaned and *wanted*. They slipped backwards onto the huge sofa and she closed her eyes as he pushed up her baggy shirt, pulling it over her head while she obligingly extended her arms to accommodate him. She had never been inhibited about her body and the removal of her shirt felt wonderful, allowed her more movement.

'You're beautiful,' he rasped huskily, and she half-opened her eyes and smiled.

'Don't talk,' she whispered and those two words sent a shiver of crazy adrenaline rushing around his body like a fever. He could feel her breathing heavily beneath him. Her breathing was an aphrodisiac. In fact, he had never felt so consumed by lust in his life before. Every experience he'd ever had with any woman now seemed like minor dress rehearsals for this one big, overwhelming experience.

Just restraining his urge to rip off the bra that barely contained her breasts was both painful and wildly intoxicating. He kissed and nibbled the thrusting swell, guiding his tongue into her cleavage and enjoying her abandoned response to his touch.

Love and lust was a heady mixture. He could feel her innocence under his fingers, innocence without the coyness which most women possessed in generous measure. She wanted him and she wasn't hardened enough to try and dissemble. He unclasped the front opening of her bra and moaned in anticipation of the pleasure he would get pulling it aside, freeing those large breasts from their imprisonment. God, he wanted to slow down—but he couldn't. His body wasn't behaving sensibly enough for any such thing.

He was only just beginning to realise how long he had wanted this woman. It felt like for ever.

He slowly pushed aside her bra and his breathing thickened as he feasted his eyes on her breasts. She didn't want talking—oh, no—and nor did he, but if he'd been inclined he could have spent at least an hour expounding on what he was looking at. Firm, big breasts with big, swollen brown nipples, each topped with protruding buds that seemed to be begging for his lips.

This he would not rush, even though his throbbing, stiff manhood, pushing against his zipped trousers, was making its demands very clear.

He bent his head to one breast and flicked his tongue over the protruding bud. This woman's body, like her company, was worth savouring. He wanted to taste every inch of her, and then he wanted to repeat the process all over again.

Her hands moved to his head, urging him to do more than just lick, and he pushed her breasts up with his hands, suckling avidly on the nipples, turned on by the sheen of his saliva on them.

He touched her stomach, placed his hand palm-down on it, and then moved to caress the inside of her thigh.

From the depths of her excitement, Destiny knew

where his hand wanted to be. She wanted it too. Her body was melting, waiting for him. Through her jeans, he began to rub, cupping her while she squirmed against his hand. She felt him undo the button of her trousers, pull down the zipper, and terror made her stiffen.

She had never made love before and this wasn't how she was supposed to lose her virginity. She struggled under him and he looked at her.

'What's the matter?'

'I can't.' They were both still breathing heavily.

'You can't?'

'I'm sorry,' she said helplessly. 'I…I've never…'

'And I'll be gentle, my darling…'

'No. You don't understand.' He had called her *his darling,* but she wasn't, was she? Cold reality gleefully resurfaced. She'd given herself, allowed him to do things, and she'd never stopped to ask herself why. *Why* the sudden physical interest in her? Well, she asked the question now and the answer came immediately. He was a man on the rebound, vulnerable and in need, and she'd been a willing and eager participant in easing his pain after Stephanie.

'What? What don't I understand? I understand what you wanted up to a minute ago…'

'This isn't right.' She wriggled, but he was already drawing back from her, sitting up, watching as she miserably fumbled with her bra, then shoved her shirt back on. Dishevelled, but at least clothed. In a manner of speaking.

'Why not?' Callum demanded. 'We're both adults.'

'I can't just… Look, I'm sorry, but…I'm not a Stephanie substitute…'

'I never accused you of being one!' he exploded; then he drew in a few sharp breaths and eyed her narrowly.

'And I can't… I have to love someone… I'm not the kind of girl who… I realise that there's an awful lot I don't know, and I'm sure if I were a bit more sophisticated…who knows…? But I'm not, and I can't, and I want to go up to my room now. Please.'

'Go ahead,' he said brusquely. 'I'm not about to stop you. But your mother should have warned you about leading men on.'

His words echoed in her head as she finally made it to her bedroom, as did the sensation of his eyes on her back as she had fled in inelegant panic.

Want and lust were all very well, but they weren't enough. She needed stability and security and marriage and babies, and if that was old-fashioned, then it described it down to the last detail.

She lay down on the bed, buried her face in her pillow and knew that she would have to do something about what was happening to her. She could feel herself poised with one foot dangling over the cliff, and she couldn't fall over.

She needed to remind herself of what was real for her and there was only one person who could do that for her.

CHAPTER SEVEN

HENRI arrived in England eight days later.

During the interim, Destiny immersed herself in the company, had daily meetings with various members of the board to discuss flow charts, saw Derek twice, had dinner with Stephanie several times and generally busied herself with anything and everything that could take her mind off Callum.

To a certain degree, it worked.

It was easier not to think of him when she was busy grappling with the complexities of profit and loss accounts and budgets which, even to her unskilled eyes, appeared horrendously optimistic. But the minute her mind wasn't occupied it slipped back to their love-making and, to the even more disastrous Sunday, when they had toured the grounds, keeping a measured distance between them and acting as though nothing had happened. He'd appeared to find that very easy to do. As he'd appeared to be relaxed around Stephanie. In fact, they had seemed more relaxed than when they'd been engaged. Maybe he had been trying to prove a point. The only point he'd ended up proving, through his silence, was that what had happened between them had been a regrettable inconvenience but not much more.

He'd only called her once since then, to find out whether she'd made any decisions about his offer, to which she'd responded with her rehearsed speech about needing a bit more time, needing to consult Derek and informing him that either she or her lawyer would be in touch as soon as possible. It had been a brilliant five-minute exercise in concealment but she'd been shaking after the telephone call.

So, right now, she was banking on Henri to restore her perspective.

When it came to Callum Ross, she seemed to spend half her time banking on someone or something to restore her perspective. She was, she'd thought ruefully, fast becoming a cast member in one of life's soap operas.

Henri emerged into the open walkway along with the rest of the passengers from his flight, trailing his suitcase on a trolley and peering anxiously around to see if he could spot her.

Destiny felt a swell of fondness, waved and gesticulated and, when she had finally made her way over to him, gathered him in a hug.

'You look different, Dessie,' he said, pushing her back to give her the once-over. '*Very smart.* Where's my little girl with the bright clothes and the scrubbed face?' He smiled warmly at her.

'She's temporarily on leave,' Destiny said, speaking in Spanish because she was beginning to feel that her bright, shiny, complicated new life was making her lose touch with the things she had always taken for granted. 'Tell me everything that's been happening on the compound. How's Dad? Has he sorted out his filing system as yet? And how's Martha and John?' She linked her arm fondly through his as they walked to the terminal exit.

She might have changed but dear Henri was still the same. Smaller and thinner than she remembered, but just as appealing, with his small round glasses and his engaging smile.

'I'm really glad you made it over, Henri,' she told him, one hour later when they were standing in the hall of her townhouse. 'Really glad that you decided to use some of your leave here instead of Paris.'

'The temptation to see little Destiny in surroundings other than a jungle was irresistible,' he said, looking around him with interest and then finally turning his attention to her. He was standing less than two feet away from her; their eyes were meeting, but she felt nothing but sisterly affection for the man whose flirting had once aroused the occasional romantic notion in her. It was nothing like what she felt when she was around Callum, the giddiness, the excitement, the feeling of *being alive*.

'And, besides, your father was worried about you,' he confessed.

'Why?' she cried, alarmed. 'Worried for what reason? Everything's going smoothly over here.'

'But you still felt desperate enough to ask me to come over.'

'I wasn't desperate. I wanted to see you. I'm not going to be here for ever and I thought it would be fun for us to see London together. That's all.'

'Sure that's all there is to it?'

'Pretty much,' Destiny mumbled, turning away towards the kitchen while he followed in her wake. 'Do you fancy something to eat? A drink? How was the flight? Are you tired? I can show you up to your bedroom if you like.'

'To answer your questions, no, yes, fine, yes and in a minute.'

But he was still curious about what was really going on with her. He allowed his curiosity to be reined in while they continued to chat about everything under the sun but the expression in his eyes when they rested on her was one of concern.

'I've arranged for you to see the medical facilities of

the company,' she told him, as they headed up to the spare room that would be his. 'I thought you might find it interesting.'

'Not, I gather, that it'll be of much use if you go ahead and sell the company.'

'I might not.' She drew his curtains, flicked her hand over the bedspread and averted her eyes. 'I've had an offer, actually. By the same man who wanted to buy the company. Callum Ross. Have I mentioned him?'

'Not even in passing since I came.'

'No? Well, he's considering helping out financially in exchange for a house in the country I've also been willed.'

'Let me get this right, Dessie... This man, whose name you've studiously avoided mentioning all evening, is proposing to pour millions into a company that's currently losing money in exchange for...a house?'

'It's a big house.'

'Sure it's just the house he wants in exchange?' There was teasing amusement in his voice. 'Sure he doesn't want *you* thrown into the bargain?'

Destiny rounded on him with vigour, hands on hips, thunderous frown on her face. 'No, he most certainly *does not want me thrown into the bargain!* That's an awful thing to say! He's *not my type* and I am very far from being *his!* In fact, the man's arrogant, bossy and pushy!'

Henri held up both his hands in mock surrender but his expression was shrewd. 'Okay! I get the message! Arrogant, bossy and pushy! Just the type of man to get on the nerves of a determined, forceful woman with a mind of her own!'

'Exactly.' She offered him a weak grin. 'Anyway, he's just broken up from my stepcousin—or, should I say, he's just been dumped by her, and not a minute too soon, as far as I'm concerned. Stephanie says it's like a weight being lifted from her shoulders, even though they're still friends.'

'You seem to have become very involved in the lives of the rich and the beautiful, Dessie... Methinks the little chick is maturing...'

'Shut up,' she laughed, 'or I'll hit you over the head with the kettle!'

'I'm cowering!'

'Anyway, you'd better get some sleep now. Tomorrow there's no time for jet lag, not when you've only got ten days over here. I've got an itinerary planned as long as my arm and in the evening we're going to the theatre with my stepcousin. She's dying to meet you.'

'Haven't been telling lies about me again, have you?' he joked. 'Like the time we went to the city and you sent me to collect a shirt you'd bought. Do you remember? Me, standing there, with a flowered blouse in my hand, and you show up and explain to the sales girl that I can't help myself but that there's nothing wrong with men wearing women's clothing if it makes them happy?'

'I was a kid at the time!'

'A kid of nineteen!'

But they ended the evening on a warm note, despite some choppy waters in the middle. Any hint of a relationship with Callum other than a business one would fly back to her father at the speed of light, and then her father *would* be worried. He'd had a long and traditional marriage to his childhood sweetheart and the thought that his daughter might be having any kind of fling with a man he'd never met and whom she barely knew would send him into a frenzy of paternal protectiveness. He'd never said so in so many words, but she knew that Henri was the sort of man her father would approve of for her. The very last would be the likes of Callum Ross.

Not, she thought, guiltily confused, that Callum Ross even entered the equation when it came to her private life. Really.

Of course, *studiously omitting to mention him* would arouse another burst of unhealthy curiosity, so she reluctantly dragged his name up a couple of times during the course of the next day, and was relieved when it was met with a casual air of indifference.

And the evening would be a doddle. They were meeting Stephanie at the theatre at six-thirty, well in time for the start of the play.

When she emerged at five forty-five in her glad rags, she was met with wolf whistles and a one-man round of wild applause.

'Gorgeous, darling, fabulous,' Henri said in an affected voice, approaching her to kiss her hand. 'Where does it all end? Can you tell me? Your father would be very proud!'

'To see me decked out like a clown?' But she laughed at the appreciative gleam in his eyes. She might feel a little clownish, but she knew that she didn't resemble one. Not in the slightest. The wardrobe which she'd initially bought with tentative reluctance, and originally worn with awkward self-consciousness, had now expanded and included a number of dresses of which her first saleswoman would have heartily approved. No more craven concealment of her legs. No more functional, loose garments to cope with stifling heat.

Now, she was wearing a dark green straight dress, caught in at the waist and reaching her mid-calves. The neckline was off the shoulder and scooped low enough to expose the first hint of cleavage. And she was in heels, something she'd never, ever worn in Panama. The heels meant that she was taller than her escort, and she wondered how she'd never noticed Henri's lack of stature before. She could see the top of his head and she had to resist the temptation to give him a quick pat.

They'd booked a taxi to take them to the theatre and they arrived to find no sign of Stephanie. In fact, there was no sign of her at all until they were seated, and then she chose to make her entrance with the panache of someone who thrived on attention. Not that you would ever think it, looking at her, because she approached their row with the vaguely lost and bewildered expression of someone not quite sure of their surroundings.

Destiny grinned wryly and could imagine how many men would be watching the beautiful brunette, wishing that they could leap to her assistance.

She turned to point her out to her companion, only to find him staring at Stephanie with an open-mouthed, befuddled expression. He watched, fascinated, as she made an apologetic fuss of having to make everyone in the row stand to allow her to pass, yet, mysteriously, was not so bothered by the disturbance as to hurry in the slightest.

Unlike Destiny's, Stephanie's dress was brief, and the palest of blue so that every inch of her small, supple body stood out in sharp contrast. The wavy hair had been tamed into perfect sleek straightness and flowed like silk around her face and over her shoulders, halfway down her back.

It was quite an entrance, Destiny thought with amusement, and if it was all part of the partner-searching game, then it was working, because Henri, once the introductions had been made, had been reduced to throat-clearing, speechless wonder.

'Remember the play?' she was forced to whisper halfway through the performance, when she could yet again feel his head staring at the averted profile of the woman sitting to the right of Destiny.

'You should have told me what she looked like,' he said in a responding whisper.

'And you would have prepared yourself by...?'

'Putting on some aftershave.'

'You're wasted as a doctor, Henri. You should be writing sex manuals—especially if your key to mutual attraction can be summed up in one word, *aftershave*.'

'Think of the money I could save all those poor men who spend their time buying flowers and chocolates.'

He fancied Stephanie. Frankly, any passing interest *they* might have had in one another had been, she suspected, the combination of their surroundings and a lack of basic choice when it came to members of the opposite sex. They understood each other and they liked one another, and occasionally that affection had manifested itself in a kiss and a cuddle, but she could see now that there had never been anything beyond that. She could feel him shifting restlessly next to her, responding to the woman on her other side, and there was no jealousy or envy, just amusement.

By the time the interval rolled round, it was a relief to get to the bar. At least there he would be able to talk to Stephanie instead of just breathing heavily and sneaking sidelong glances every three seconds.

But did he talk? Stephanie talked—talked with that animated, endearing eagerness that made her such a warm person. Destiny talked about how wonderful it was to be at the theatre for the first time, about the little plays she'd used to get her children at the school to do, dramatisations of the classics she had read over the years. But Henri could barely manage to piece together three sentences without displaying all the signs of a man bowled over by the sight of a woman.

In the end, it was Stephanie and not Destiny who saved the situation.

'I don't want to intrude on anything you two might have going…' She raised her eyebrows expressively at the both of them, and, while Destiny firmly denied any such thing, Henri stuttered out his version of the same. 'But I'd really like to get to know you, Henri…' She lifted his spectacles gently and smiled at his confusion. 'And this is utterly the wrong place. Too many people, too much going on…'

'We can leave,' he said eagerly. 'Go somewhere for a bite to eat…' In his haste, he slipped partially back into his native French and Stephanie looked delighted.

'We can't leave Destiny here by herself,' Stephanie said quietly, at which point the bell rang and Destiny took matters into her own hands. She had never played matchmaker in her life before, but there was a first for everything, and how much could there be in it?

'You two *go*. I'm perfectly capable of enjoying the rest of this performance on my own, and I booked a taxi to collect us after the play. I'll find my way home.'

'Destiny!' Henri looked mildly shocked. 'Taxi? You're—'

'Independent, Henri,' she said, smiling, as the bell rang again and the bar began to clear. 'I was independent in Panama and I'm independent here. You can't keep a capable girl down.'

'But…'

'Come on, Henri.' Stephanie caught him by the tie and tugged him gently, at which he obediently fell into line with her. Only as Destiny was leaving the bar herself did

Stephanie run up breathlessly to say, 'Had to tell you, Dessie. That felt so *good!*'

'What did?'

'Being the one to call the shots!' She dashed back out, pausing to wave at Destiny, and then they disappeared.

The performance had restarted by the time Destiny made her way back to the empty seats, head down in embarrassment at everyone having to shift sideways or lever themselves up to let her through, and it was only when she was sitting that a dark, velvety voice said from one seat along,

'Hope you don't mind if I join you?'

'What are you doing here?'

The question was ignored as Callum shifted one seat along so that he was directly next to her, his elbow resting on the divide between them.

'What are you doing here?' she repeated tensely. The perspective angle hadn't worked at all. In fact, it had monumentally backfired, and she could feel that surge of emotion hit her like a sledgehammer as she glared at his averted profile and breathed in his masculine smell that had nothing to do with aftershave of any description.

'Shh, the play.' He settled back into his seat, while next to him she seethed and tried to figure out how Fate could be malignant enough to throw him into her company at this precise moment in time.

'Aren't you enjoying it?' he murmured in a low voice, 'I can feel you bristling next to me like a steam engine about to explode.'

'I *was* enjoying it.'

'Oh, you mean until I came along.' He didn't appear to be disconcerted by that, and when she opened her mouth again his response was to say, 'Shh!'

So she found herself sitting through the remainder of

the play, which had lost its appeal, while questions piled up in her head. But she restrained herself from saying another word until the performance was ended, the encores had been done and the lights were on. She was barely aware of the crowds of people surging past her towards the exit. Nor was she about to look around to see whether Callum was behind her. In fact, she'd almost convinced herself that he had somehow got lost in the crowd, perhaps even trampled underfoot, when she felt the pressure of his hand on her elbow.

'So where to now?'

'*I've* got a taxi booked...'

'Oh, good. Mind if I grab a lift with you? Taxis can be hell to come by at this hour outside a theatre.' He followed her outside, meekly allowing her to stride towards her taxi, head held high, but once they were inside the car, he turned and said, 'Where were you planning to eat?'

Originally, she wanted to ask, *or now that my escort's vanished?* Then it dawned on her that he was probably aware of exactly why she had been sitting in a row of three on her own. He must have seen her from the start, or else how would he have known where she was sitting? The thought that he'd been watching her made the hairs on the back of her neck tingle. Watching and...laughing?

'Actually, I thought I might just go home and give food a miss,' Destiny said in a stiff, polite voice, head carefully averted.

'*Give food a miss? You?*'

That made her snap round to look at him, although she had a sneaking suspicion that that had been the intention when he had made his gibe.

'I do occasionally skip food,' she told him with glacier-like formality, but the ice in her voice was ambushed by her wide, dilated pupils and for a few heady seconds she was held hostage by his piercing, sexy blue eyes.

It was, he thought, like an attempt to quench a roaring furnace with three drips of water, a token, desperate effort to distance him, and the awareness of that filled him with a crude, primitive sense of triumph. That tentative taste of her one week ago had been like a tantalising aperitif. It had stirred a hunger in him that had been shockingly erotic and one week of absence had done nothing to still it.

Love and animal lust swelled inside him, making his groin ache, and he struggled to let none of it show on his face. The slightest smell of his desire would send her running a mile. In all his life he'd never wanted a woman the way he wanted her, and it was just his luck that she was the one woman whose traditional, principled outlook was like a steel barrier between them.

'Not tonight.' He leaned towards the taxi driver and gave him an address, then he sat back and waited for her inevitable question, which was not long in coming.

'Where are we going?'

'Just a little place I know where we can get something light to eat.'

He sat back against the door and watched her. Watching her gave him a peculiar feeling of pleasure. Watching her, absorbing the expressions that flitted across her face. Even now, as she turned away, hunching her shoulder like someone trying to fend off danger through body language, he still enjoyed the view. Her skin was like satin, smooth and brown, making her hair look even richer and blonder in comparison. He wanted to reach out and gather it up between his fingers, so that he could pull her closer to him. He imagined her weight against him and the bird's-eye view he would have of the enticing swell of her breasts, barely restrained by her low-cut neckline. She had a body that always appeared to be bursting to get out of the clothes she wrapped around it.

That little wimp she had brought with her to the theatre was no match for her. She needed a man, a *real* man. Him, in other words. And she damned well knew it. It was written in every word she didn't say and in every expression she tried so hard to conceal.

Henri. That was his name. Callum had met Stephanie the evening before; their conversation had no longer been strained by the invisible pressure hanging over their heads that they were an engaged couple, and should therefore be frantic to climb into the nearest convenient bed, and he'd managed to pump a fair amount of information out of her.

They would discuss this Henri character just as soon as they had reached their destination. He was pretty good at reading body language, and from what he had glimpsed mutual sexual attraction had not been on the agenda, but still, they had appeared relaxed with one another—and relaxed was always a bad sign.

'Is this a restaurant?' Her voice broke through his reverie and he realised that the taxi had stopped and she was now looking past him to his townhouse.

'In a manner of speaking.' He opened his door, paid the driver, leaving a generous tip and waited impatiently for her to exit the taxi.

'What do you mean, "in a manner of speaking"?'

'I mean there's food inside.' He hustled her along, preparing himself for the inevitable explosion—which occurred just as soon as she was through his front door.

'It's your house, isn't it?' She turned to him, her cheeks flushed with colour.

Instead of answering, he calmly switched on the hall light. 'How do you like it?'

'You brought me to your house! You told me that we were going to a restaurant!'

'I did no such thing,' he demurred. 'I told you that I knew somewhere we could get something light to eat.'

'You lied! I demand to be dropped back to my house! Immediately!'

'Why?'

'Why? *Why?* Because—'

'Promise...no touching...' He held up both hands, palms towards her. 'At least, not unless you want me to...' he added very softly to himself. 'Food and a bit of business. I need to wrap this matter up with the company within the week.'

'You do?' Destiny asked hesitantly. 'Why? You never mentioned a deadline for my decision.'

'Business runs on deadlines,' Callum informed her, improvising as he went along and managing to usher her into the kitchen while she ruminated over what he had said. 'I have my board breathing down my neck, wanting to know whether we'll be acquiring Felt's. My accountants need to know how to distribute the money with year-end coming up.'

'But I can't *give* you an answer,' she said from behind him, while he started extracting pots and pans and cooking ingredients from various cupboards and the fridge.

'Why not? What's the problem? I'm offering to practically bail you out.' Now that he'd managed to get her into the kitchen, it seemed as safe a policy as any not to focus his attention on her. She had forgotten that she'd been brought to his house against her will. No point reminding her of the fact by trying to stare her down.

'Yes, well...' She shuffled over to the kitchen table,

which was constructed of wood and chrome and was very high-tech-looking, and ran her hands over the smooth surface. She sighed and looked at him as he chopped vegetables and expertly tossed things in a frying pan. Whatever he was cooking, there were some very reassuring smells emanating from it.

'Do you need any help?' she asked awkwardly.

'No. Just sit. I'm fully capable of cooking a simple meal for two without help. Don't guarantee how it's going to taste, but it'll be better than nothing.'

'Smells good,' Destiny said politely, raising her voice to compensate for the sound of sizzling, then she lapsed into silence, content to look.

Within ten minutes he began fishing plates out and allowed her to lend a hand by laying the table.

'Now, eat and enjoy,' he commanded when he was finally sitting opposite her with the overhead light dimmed—which he had jokingly told her was a famous ruse of the uncertain chef, who preferred to spare his audience too much clarity when it came to his food.

'It tastes…delicious.' There was a lot of pasta, and he had stir fried vegetables with cream and parmesan cheese which soaked into the noodles like gravy.

'Good. So…I couldn't help noticing at the theatre that you arrived with a man… Looked a nice guy… Who was he? Friend of Steph's?'

'How did you manage to pick us out among all those people?'

'I think everyone in the place noticed Stephanie when she walked in five minutes after everyone was seated. Must have been a bit embarrassing arriving on time with her chap, to find that she hadn't arrived yet…'

'Actually, Henri's staying with me,' Destiny said reluctantly. 'He works with me in Panama and I invited him over for a few days.'

'Oh. *I* get the picture. Bad luck for you. He seemed besotted with my ex—and, of course, he left with her during the interval, didn't he?'

'Were you *spying* on us?' Destiny asked abruptly. 'If you're still that obsessed with Stephanie, then I suggest you tell her—because you might find that someone else is around to pick up the pieces!'

'I wasn't *spying* on you and, believe me, you couldn't be further from the truth as far as my feelings for Stephanie go. I'm more than happy that someone will pick up the pieces—not that there are any pieces to pick up. I'm just sorry that the man in question happens to be *your* man.'

'Henri is not *my* man! He's a friend! Some of us *do* have friends of the opposite sex, in case you hadn't noticed!'

'A very good friend, from the looks of it...'

'So you *were* spying on us!'

'I happened to see you at the start of the play and naturally I found myself glancing over every so often!'

'Who were you there with, anyway?' Destiny asked suspiciously.

'Office people. Finished eating?' He cleared away the table and had to deliver a stern lecture to himself to lighten up. Hadn't she told him what he had already known? That the wimp with the spectacles was nothing more than a friend? Yes. Then why did he still feel jealous? Course, he knew why. He felt jealous because she had admitted that he was a good friend, and now his head was rife with images of them sharing long, intimate conversations, the likes of which she would never share with *him* because she viewed everything he said and did with a liberal pinch of suspicion.

'No dessert,' he said brusquely. 'Sorry.'

'I'll help you wash up.'

'Don't bother.'

'It's no bother.' She came to the kitchen sink and stood next to him, waiting till he filled a bowl with warm, soapy water. His kitchen overlooked a private back garden, now wreathed in darkness. It was far more private than where she was living but, on the other hand, it was also further out of central London, which was much nicer, she thought. Quieter, less frantic. Large French doors led out of the kitchen into the back garden, so that there was an impression of airiness about the room.

'You don't expect me to believe that you and this…man…are…were…*just good friends,* do you? Despite what you say about having friends of the opposite sex, you're a big girl. You must know that such a thing doesn't exist.' Instead of washing, he plunged both his hands into the soapy water and stared at the distorted image they created.

He shouldn't be pursuing this. He knew that she wasn't involved with the man sexually. Dammit, he had eyes in his head and had seen all the signs for himself, but he wanted to hear her say that Henri meant nothing to her. He wanted to be told that he was more interesting, more engaging than his bespectacled and unknowing rival.

Destiny didn't say anything and he turned to look at her, wondering whether she'd even heard what he'd asked. He found her looking right back at him, her green eyes curious and comprehending.

'Are you *jealous* of Henri?' she asked in a faltering voice, at which he forced a bark of laughter out.

'Me? *Jealous?* I've never been jealous of anyone in my entire life and I certainly don't intend to start now!'

The blue eyes that met hers were fiercely proud, but she *knew.* She knew that he had been jealous, even if his jealousy was only based on the sheer egotistical physical grounds of not liking the idea that someone else might have touched her when he was still interested, and the knowledge made her heart flutter wildly inside her.

She wanted to tell him that there was no need, that she'd only ever loved one man and that was him. The admission whipped the breath from her throat and she stared back glassily at him, her lips slightly apart. She turned away, but not before he'd seen that brief flash of hunger that mirrored his own.

'Does it make you feel good?' he taunted softly. 'That a big, strong man like me might be reduced to a pitiful emotion like jealousy?' He lifted one hand out of the water and swung her head to face him. One side of her face was now wet and slippery.

'Yes,' she threw back honestly. 'It makes me feel good.'

Now both hands were out of the water and cupping her face, stroking her cheekbones, and she could feel all her good intentions disintegrating like sand through a strainer. She couldn't fight him any more. What she felt was powerful enough to destroy every item in the feeble armoury she had in reserve. She was sick of looking at him and wanting to touch him and telling herself that she shouldn't, that it was wrong. She was sick of being scared and out of her depth. She loved him and she wanted him and if he was only aware of one of those two things, then that was enough. She would leave England all too soon. Why leave with regrets for things undone?

She ran the tip of her tongue over her lips, aware of the rampantly sexual come-on signal she was giving and, when he bent his head towards hers with a groan, she sighed and offered herself to him with abandonment.

CHAPTER EIGHT

'WHY don't we leave all these dirty dishes and go upstairs?' he murmured into her ear, and she gave a whimper in response. She really didn't care where they were, just so long as she could feel his hard body pressed against hers.

They walked up the stairs to his bedroom, with Destiny noticing absolutely nothing on the way. If someone had asked her what the colour of the wallpaper was on the walls, or whether she was walking on carpet, wooden flooring, tiles or red hot coals, for that matter, she would not have been able to give an answer. In fact, she felt as though she were floating, and his fingers laced through hers were like fire against her skin.

By the time they finally made it to his bedroom she knew that she was shaking like a leaf, a combination of excitement and nerves, and she raised her eyes hesitantly to his. At the door, she paused wordlessly.

'I suppose you must be accustomed to this...sort of thing...' Her voice was barely above a whisper and he gazed at her softly.

'I'm not celibate, if that's what you mean. And there's no need to be scared...'

'You don't mind that... I mean, with all your experience... Does it bother you that I'm a...?'

'Virgin?'

Destiny nodded, blushing at the bluntness of the word, now that it was out in the open. Never in a million years would she have imagined that her own lack of experience would have left her feeling so vulnerable. She could stop right now; she knew that. Call a halt and walk right back down those stairs. But she also knew that she wouldn't. This was *right*.

'I have never felt so honoured in my life,' he said huskily, which brought an unsteady smile to her lips. 'Come with me.' He led her into the massive *en suite* bathroom and then sat her down in a wicker chair by the window.

'What are you doing?'

'I'm going to relax you.'

She watched as he began running a bath, testing the temperature every so often with his fingers, adding bubble bath that smelt of cinnamon. The bath was grand enough to suit the dimensions of the bathroom. It was a Victorian masterpiece, with clawed feet. A large, masculine bath that blended well with the forest-green and white tiles surrounding it. She could easily imagine him lying in it, long, indolent, one arm draped lazily over the side, eyes closed. And, of course, naked.

The thought made her pulses begin to race once more.

What, she thought a little hysterically, did one do with a man's naked body? Would he be as big and awesome *down there* as his build suggested? She was so lacking in experience that she doubted she would know what to touch. The idea made her feel faint and she closed her eyes briefly.

'Not dozing off, are you?'

Her eyes flew open to find him standing above her, smiling.

'No,' she squeaked, gripping the arms of the wicker chair.

'Stand up.'

Destiny obeyed. Without saying so, she knew that he

was well aware of the battle raging between her fear at stepping into the unknown and her excitement at the prospect, and he was taking control. She also knew that she could trust him implicitly.

'Now, my darling, just you stand there...' He gently kissed her eyes and stroked her eyebrows with his thumbs.

If only she knew what agony it was, he thought to himself. If only she knew that he was damned nervous himself, though not of the physical act, as she was. Understandably. No, he just wanted to touch her everywhere and in every way that would be right for her, make her the recipient of his glorious passion and feel that body of hers respond to his the way he knew she would. There was something touchingly childlike about this tall woman who could tackle anything life threw at her but this.

He rolled his fingers along her collarbone and very slowly began to undo the long zipper at the back of her dress, feeling her quick, shallow breathing under his hands. It slipped to the ground and pooled around her ankles. God, he was trembling almost as much as she was! He moved to unclasp her bra from the front.

Her breasts spilled out in all their bounty.

He could feel urgency and hunger hit his loins with gut-wrenching force and he forced himself to breathe deeply and evenly. Given his way, he would ravish her right here and now, on the bathroom floor, and, God, he probably wouldn't even have time to strip himself of all his clothes, but she was like a thoroughbred filly that needed to be treated with the utmost care.

The bra was tossed onto the black ash linen basket. Her head was thrown back and her rapid breathing made her chest fall and rise. Her nipples were large and erect, waiting to be touched. And touched they would be, but not yet. He would wait for her to come to him.

The bathroom light was on a dimmer switch, and he had dimmed it so that no harsh light invaded the room. Instead, gentle shadows washed over them with every small movement.

Her body was perfectly toned. Of course, he knew that—had fantasised about it for the nightmarishly long week that had stretched between them since he had last seen her—but, still, seeing her standing in front of him made him feel winded. Naked, with her large breasts resting against her ribcage, the slender waist, beneath which dipped the elastic band of her underwear.

He knelt in front of her and it momentarily flashed through his head that in every respect she had brought him to his knees. Then he curled one finger on either side of her briefs and peeled them down. This time he had to close his eyes and steady himself. Just for a second. Just long enough to get himself and his throbbing body back into some kind of control. He inhaled deeply, breathing in her womanhood, then ran his hands lightly up either side of her thighs, enjoying it as she shuddered beneath him.

'Bath time,' he murmured, standing up.

'Already? Must I?'

'It'll relax you.'

'I feel relaxed already,' Destiny said, tentatively placing her hand on his cheek, then running it up through his dark hair.

'You haven't begun to relax yet,' he promised softly, and she obediently climbed into the water, which was at a perfect temperature. Warm and so full of bubbles that her body was obscured by them.

He slipped round to the back of the bath and for a few

minutes transported her to bliss as he kneaded the muscles at the back of her neck and along her shoulders.

The tips of her hair, hanging in the water, were damp and darker than the halo of blonde he breathed into, kissing the nape of her neck, then he moved and lathered his hands with soap.

This time he didn't have to tell her what to do. She stood up, wet, with an expression of pleasure on her face. When he began sliding his soapy hands along her shoulders and arms, she smiled with the languid contentment of a cat.

The thought of running his hands over her breasts produced such feelings of exquisite anticipation in him that he almost wanted to delay the moment for as long as possible.

But they were waiting for him, like fruit waiting to be savoured, and savour them he did, massaging the soap over them, drawing the pouting nipples to throbbing hardness, while she moaned unsteadily. Then along the flat planes of her stomach, along her thighs and finally, with slow, rhythmic strokes, over the mound of her femininity. He felt it pulsate under the palm of his hand and ran a finger along the crease, finding the nub which he stroked until her moaning became faster and hoarser.

Rinsing off the soap was something she did in record time, and now his hunger was ripening into a steady throb. He dried her and led her into his bedroom and onto the king-sized bed with its tan and terracotta duvet and puffy pillows.

She felt a fleeting sense of wonder at what she was knowingly about to step into. The great big unknown. And then a twinge of alarm that for all her reasoning about enjoying this while it lasted, she was about to jump off a precipice and the fall might prove fatal.

It didn't last long. She lay on the bed, naked and beyond the point of turning back, and watched him greedily as he removed his clothes.

The body she'd imagined was even more impressive than the vague picture she'd conjured up in her newly, irrepressibly fertile head.

Every inch of him was tautly muscled. His limbs were aggressively long and athletic. He watched her watching him and smiled lazily, enjoying her obvious pleasure afforded by the view.

'Let's take our time,' he murmured, when he was lying on his side next to her, their faces almost touching. 'The best things in life need to be savoured for the longest possible time.' He kissed her gently, delicately almost, his tongue licking the contours of her mouth then invading it with supreme thoroughness. Destiny, already on the brink, cradled his head with her hands, then arched back to enjoy the slow path of his mouth as it nibbled and licked her shoulders, finally reaching her aching breasts.

He levered his powerful body over hers, supporting himself with his arms, and devoted all his attention to her full breasts, stroking them with his tongue, sucking the nipples into his mouth, arousing her until she wanted to cry out for satisfaction.

When his head moved inexorably down, so that his exploration of her body could be complete, she thought that she might faint with the intense pleasure of it.

He parted her willing thighs, then after a few teasing nuzzles into the soft down of her hair, he buried his face against her and she gave a little cry of ecstasy as his tongue found its spot and pressed on it in small flicking motions.

Her body seemed to be moving of its own accord. How could she ever have worried that she *wouldn't know what to do?* She raised her hips and curled her fingers into his hair, pushing him down against her, writhing to accommodate his mouth. With wanton lack of inhibition, she rolled the palms of her hands over her nipples, stimulating them, while the lower half of her body continued to do its amazing, erotic dance.

He wasn't about to give her the isolated satisfaction of an orgasm now, though. He could feel mounting need, but before it crested he pulled away, and replaced his mouth with his own fullness, inserting himself gently; after a moment of rigidity, she bucked frantically against him, taking him in and panting as they both came to a shuddering climax.

There was no embarrassment when he eased himself off her and lay next to her, propping himself up on his elbows so that he could inspect her flushed, satisfied face.

Destiny had never felt so free in her life before. Some measure of reason was beginning to set in, but she felt no regrets. Just complete and utter joy that her first act of lovemaking had been with the man she loved. Never mind that he wasn't aware of the fact and never would be. In her own head, and in her heart, she'd not betrayed herself.

'That was…' she said drowsily, searching for just the right word, '…exquisite.'

'Ditto…' He kissed the tip of her nose.

'Don't fib,' she chastised teasingly. 'I didn't *do* anything…'

'How can you say that? The proof of what you did was right in front of your eyes! Not to mention in other parts as well…' He gave a slow, sexy chuckle. 'And, in a very short while, there'll be more ample proof of what you do to me clamouring for a bit more of the same…'

'Will there?' Her green eyes widening innocently. 'Or are you just saying that to make me feel good…?'

'Of course, I *do* want you to feel good—' he stroked her legs then dipped his fingers to slide gracefully over her wetness '—and I think I've succeeded…but I think my little beauty needs a rest before…we rediscover each other's bodies…'

'Never mind a rest…I could do with a shower. Would it be all right if I had one?'

'Only if it would be all right if I joined you…'

Later, fresh after a shower which had taken much longer than any of the showers she'd ever had on the compound, due to a mutual lack of conviction that getting out was the object of the exercise, they found themselves back in the kitchen and confronting the forgotten pile of unwashed dishes.

With a bit of imagination, Destiny found that she could create her own little bubble, in which this wonderful domesticity, alongside the man she loved, would be longlasting. He washed the dishes while she dried them, and their conversation was lazy, relaxed, teasing and utterly unlike what she would have imagined having with this man only weeks previously.

Whoever said that love needed time to flourish? And with all the right environmental conditions? It was more like a weed, capable of sprouting forth in the most hostile of places and, once sprouted, of growing with rapid and tenacious speed.

'I guess I'd better be getting back home,' she said reluctantly, when all the dishes were dried. She neatly placed the cloth over the rail of the Aga and felt him move up behind her until his hands were on her waist and his chin nestled against the crook of her shoulder.

'Why?'

'Why what? Why should I leave?'

'Why *should* you leave?' he murmured provocatively. 'When there's so much left for us to do…? Bit difficult to make love when we're miles apart, isn't it? And I've never been much of a fan of telephone sex… Always seemed like a recipe for frustration to me, although it has to be said that getting dirty down the end of line might have a few attractions…' He slipped his hand underneath the shirt she had borrowed from him and cupped one of her breasts, jiggling it so that it bounced gently against his palm. 'I love your nipples. They're so…' He nibbled her earlobe, sending little shivers of delight racing down her spine, and she leant languorously back against him.

'Big. Everything about me is big,' she said with a little laugh.

'And does that bother you?'

'Not really.' She shrugged and thought about it. 'Sometimes I used to feel a bit awkward at having to talk down to all the other women on the compound, but on the whole it's been to my advantage. If you can call it an advantage to be opted for all the more physical jobs that require a bit of strength.' Now his hands caressed both her breasts, pausing only to rub thumbs over the peaks of her nipples now and again. She felt a familiar stirring down below. The kind of stirring that turned her brain to cotton wool.

'You mean the bespectacled Henri didn't rush to your immediate aid?'

'Doesn't work that way out there, I'm afraid. Women need to be able to do their job usefully and not rely on a man to pull them out of uncomfortable conditions.'

He paused in what he was doing. 'Was your mother as capable as you?'

'If not more.' She sighed. 'My father said that he loved her from the very first moment he set eyes on her.'

'Where did they meet? At a dance? Dinner party?'

'Oh, she was stitching up a young boy whose head had been busted open by a cricket ball.'

'Ah. Unusual circumstances for love at first sight.'

'I guess their eyes met over the needle and nylon.' She giggled.

'So what are you going to do? Stay or stay?'

'Stay?'

'Right choice…'

Was it, though?

She had no idea what time they had finally drifted to sleep. She only knew that she was considerably more experienced in the ways of pleasuring a man than she had been at the start of the evening. And when she wakened several hours later, with needles of light filtering through the curtains, it took her several seconds to remember where she was. Then her eyes flew open to find herself alone on the bed with a mass of crumpled sheets around her.

With the cold light of day came the cold light of reality. Her fragile reasons for sleeping with Callum Ross now seemed ludicrous and naïve. Seductive words and dim lighting, and the overwhelming recognition of her own feelings for him, had worked in devilish ways to banish her reserve, and the prospect of a headlong collision with planet Earth now seemed something that couldn't be reasoned away into non-existence.

What could she have been thinking of?

Had she imagined that she could enjoy the fruition of her love for one night—or maybe one week or even one month, until she left the country—and then take off with her heart and soul intact? What was the remainder of her life going to be now? Back in Panama, with only her memories for bitter company?

She groaned silently to herself, wondering if there was any reasonable chance that she could sneak out of the house without being caught. Perhaps shinny out of the window or something.

She tried to picture someone of her stature *shinnying* and ran up against a mental block. Shinny down and break her back by crashing thunderously onto the ground in the process would be more like it.

The thing that really scared her was the suspicion that, whatever qualms were now dawning on the horizon, she would still forfeit reason for the pleasure of being with him, and she knew that the more snatched moments of happiness she stole now, the greater would be her eventual prison sentence.

The thoughts were still churning over in her mind when the object of them returned to the bedroom, wearing a white bathrobe underneath which was nothing but his bare body, as she could see every time it swung apart in rhythm with his tread.

'Breakfast,' he said, raising the tray in both hands slightly and grinning. 'Full English.' He deposited the tray on the bed, relieved himself of his bathrobe with an enviable lack of self-consciousness, then slid next to her.

On the tray was a plate heaped with bacon, sausages, toast and scrambled egg, two cups of coffee and two plates with the required cutlery stacked on top of them.

Her onslaught of misgivings evaporated at the sight of him, as she had known it would.

'Tuck in,' he said, heaping a bit of everything on a plate and sliding a spare tray from underneath onto her lap.

'Don't tell me. You're an expert at entertaining women in your bed in the morning.'

'On the contrary. Don't forget, Steph and I were together for two years and I'm a one-woman man.'

'Did you ever love her?' She took a sip of the coffee and waited for his answer.

Love her? Callum almost laughed. Love was anything but the placid affection he had felt for his former fiancée. Love, as he could now testify, was something that took over every pore of your body and left a strong man hesitant and exposed.

'We had fun for a while,' he said slowly, wishing that she was opposite him so that he could read the expression on her face. Her voice implied nothing but a casual interest. 'And I was very fond of her. I still am.'

Just like you're having fun with me for a while? she wanted to ask. Instead, she chickened out of the sickening prospect of putting him in a spot. She wondered whether that would be his future dismissal of her when he was lying on the same bed, bringing breakfast up for another woman.

She ate some of her breakfast in silence, then manoeuvred the tray onto the low oak chest of drawers next to her side of the bed.

'That was good,' she said. 'Thank you very much. The last time I had food delivered to me on a tray in my room was years ago, when I was ill, and my father waited on me hand and foot for a few days. I remember thinking at the time how nice it was not to have to fetch and carry for other people.'

She lay back against the pillow and stared up at the ceiling, feeling the bed shift as he disposed of his own tray then turned on his side to her.

'You're quite something, Destiny Felt, do you know

that?' He pulled the sheet a few inches down so that her breasts were exposed, but he didn't touch her, contenting himself with looking, until his looks were as heady as his touch would have been.

She turned to lie on her side, facing him, half wanting to cover herself, but the desire to do that was a lot less strong than the desire to watch him react to her. She had never known that one man's hunger could be such a powerful aphrodisiac. Eventually, he couldn't resist, and he trailed a finger to circle her nipple, touching it with butterfly lightness, watching as it stiffened and puckered under his finger.

'We need never stop this, you know,' he said gravely, addressing her responding breast, and her breath caught in her throat.

Wasn't this what she had wanted to hear? Some talk of commitment? Of permanence? What else could he mean? They had spent a wonderful night together, and at least as far as she was concerned it was much more than that. Somehow it felt as though their personalities fused. Did he feel it too?

She was no liberated westerner who could gaily conduct an affair as a *fun thing* while it lasted. She was a traditionalist and, although she'd slept with him, she wanted so much more.

She could feel herself holding her breath as she looked at him.

'What, not even to eat or have a bath?' she asked lightly, while her heart pounded like a steam engine inside her. Having Callum at her side, her husband, would raise a few problems—not least those concerning country of residence—but the doubts were soothed as soon as they surfaced. She would be at his side, wherever that might turn out to be.

'I'm being serious.' He lay flat on his back with his hands folded behind his head. He could feel a muscle pulsing gently in his jaw and a light film of perspiration was breaking out over his body. It hadn't been like this with Stephanie, but, then again, he hadn't been toying with his heart then. She'd wanted proof of security and he'd had no trouble agreeing to an engagement because he had felt more real warmth and affection for her than he had ever felt for any of his previous women. Not that talk of marriage had ever cropped up before. It had been something he had purposefully avoided.

But now it was different. He couldn't envisage *not* having this woman by his side for the duration of his life, for better or for worse and all those other vows uttered during a marriage ceremony, vows that he had never given much thought to in the past. And he didn't want an engagement.

But, for all that, the thought of exposing himself and telling her how he felt sent a chill of terror crawling along his veins.

It hadn't escaped him that not once during their love-making had the word *love* been mentioned, not even when she'd been flushed and moaning with pleasure, with every defence down and her head thrown back in aban-don. And that in itself said it all. Because, however sharp she was in every conceivable practical area, when it came to emotions she was still finding her way, and there was an openness there that was almost innocent in its dem-onstrations.

But, God, he still wanted her to be his for ever.

'We could get married,' he said, still staring upwards. 'I mean, it makes sense, don't you think? We're com-patible in bed—more than compatible—and it could sort out every niggling area of all this bargaining we've been trying to do over the past few weeks. I can't personally think of a better arrangement than marriage.'

She couldn't fail to see the sense behind his proposal, he thought, and then he would have time on his side. Time to woo her into loving him. He was her first lover and, in a life in which relationships had never made an imprint, she probably wasn't very certain *what* love was. She would only ever have had the example of her parents, and from the sound of it they had been an exceptional couple, both scientists, both fiercely determined to bring their skill and knowledge to a country that needed it. From the start they had been unified in their goals. But with him, well, hadn't it all been a little different?

'Arrangement?' Destiny asked numbly.

'Partnership,' he corrected quickly.

'I'm not sure,' she said, feeling cold all over and very sure indeed. Very sure that the proposition he had put to her had not been the one her romantic, delusional mind had conjured up. Now, it made her feel ill to think that she'd imagined a marriage proposal to have been made with some declaration of love, or at least with some emotion other than the coolly logical one he was displaying now.

She had to get out of here. She couldn't afford to let him start working on her with his arguments of common sense and practicality. He weakened her, and she wouldn't enter into a marriage for all the wrong reasons. That would be a recipe for disaster. Hadn't she made one disastrous error already by sleeping with him and telling herself that it was fine because she loved him? No way would she compound the mistake by adding yet another, and one that she would have a lifetime to regret.

'I need to think it over.'

'What's there to think over?' He rolled to his side and looked at her, his blue eyes urgent and demanding.

She wriggled back a bit. 'I need a few days. Just to get my head around it…to adjust…'

'Adjust to what?'

'We barely know each other!'

'We have been as intimate as two people can be…'

'That's not what I mean.' She edged towards the side of the bed and practically fell off, reaching down for her clothes and sticking on the shirt she had borrowed with her back to him.

'Where are you going?' It was more of a demand than a question. He could feel her ebbing away from him, but the temptation to push harder was something he knew he had to resist. The ebb would turn into outright flight if he did that. She said she needed time, and there was nothing ominous about that. Of course she needed time. Marriage proposals were not things that were sprung on a daily basis. The best thing he could do now would be to curb his savage impatience and let her have the time she needed. With restrictions.

'I need to get back to my place,' she mumbled, not looking at him.

Callum sprang out of bed and pulled a tee-shirt over his powerful torso, followed by boxer shorts.

'You'll need a lift back. I'll drive you.' He kept one eye on her while putting on a pair of trousers, not bothering with a belt so that they hung slightly down his hips. She had sailed into the bathroom, shutting the door, and he waited with increasing frustration for her outside, drumming his fingers on the windowsill.

One desperate part of him was beginning to think that somewhere along the line his impeccably tempting offer, full of the sort of practical advantages that would appeal to someone as clear-headed as she was, was going badly wrong.

And with the desperation, nauseating in itself because it was just so alien to him, came a rush of surly defensiveness. Shouldn't she have jumped to his offer with alacrity? Maybe, he thought, she was disturbed at the thought of cutting ties with the country she'd spent most of her life in. Perhaps she just needed time to sort out the practicalities of the issue.

That line of thought was reassuring, and by the time she emerged from the bathroom, inappropriately clad in her dress, he was prepared to be magnanimous.

'Look,' he said sympathetically, 'I understand that you might be having a few doubts about leaving Panama...' She was virtually scuttling out of the room and down the stairs, running her fingers through her uncombed hair, sticking on her shoes when she got to the front door. 'But you would be able to go over there on holiday whenever you wanted. And of course your father could come and visit whenever he wanted...'

'Oh, yes, right,' she answered in a vaguely surprised voice. She still wasn't looking at him and he positioned himself in front of the door so that she was compelled to look up. 'I hadn't really considered that aspect of it,' she continued, flushing.

'Then *what* aspects are you considering?' he demanded with a trace of aggression in his voice, and she immediately pulled away into herself.

'Please don't push me.'

'I'm not pushing you.'

'You expect me to give you a yes or no answer right this minute...'

'I *told* you I can more than understand that you might need time to think it over,' Callum said repressively.

He steadied himself and stood aside to open the door, following her into the car and starting it with barely contained anger.

'I'm going to be away for the next few days,' he said into the lengthening silence. 'So I won't be around to pester you. Do you think you might have an answer for me by the time I get back?'

'I guess I might,' Destiny told him vaguely.

'You *guess?*'

'All right, then. I will.'

'That's better.'

But when she sneaked a glance at his profile, it was grimly tight. She knew what was niggling him. He'd tossed his proposal to her, expecting her to not be able to resist. A marriage of good sex and good business, without the tricky business of love getting in the way. It made perfect sense, didn't it? And, into the bargain, she would have the pleasure of being wed to the most eligible bachelor in London and all the consequent advantages of limitless money. He must be thinking that the alternative was slinking back to Panama to continue working in a funless vacuum with enough money to fairly do what she wanted, but without the vital medical facilities the company would offer—because she knew that selling the company was virtually a foregone conclusion, despite the fact that so many people would prefer her not to go down that road.

Marriage would be of mutual benefit. He would get the company he had craved, a company that would establish a foothold in the huge, complex world of pharmaceuticals, and she in return would get the benefit of his considerable investments to make it work. Everyone would be happy.

'How long are you planning on being out of the country?' she asked tentatively, and he relaxed fractionally.

'Five days. Maybe a bit longer. Depends on how many problems I have to sort out. Why, will you miss me?'

'Will *you* miss *me?*' She threw the question back at him and felt a treacherous sense of arousal as his mouth curved into a satisfied smile.

'What do you think? Perhaps,' he drawled softly, 'I should find a deserted back road somewhere and stop the car so that I can demonstrate exactly how much I'll be missing you...'

'I don't think so,' Destiny said hurriedly, recognising the familiar road down which all her good intentions tended to go wildly astray.

'No, maybe a little absence is good for the soul.'

A little absence? He was so sure of getting what he wanted, the way he always had, all through his life.

She didn't dare contemplate his shock when he returned from his trip abroad.

'Maybe it is,' she repeated sadly.

CHAPTER NINE

CALLUM stared out of the window of his office which offered an uninspiring view of leaden skies pressing heavily above the grey, claustrophobic confines of the city. He had a meeting in under an hour and he was toying with the notion of delegating it to one of his directors, even though delegation was beginning to become something of a habit—and a habit that was not going unobserved by several of the people who worked for him.

Frankly, he didn't give a damn.

He spun round on his chair and buzzed through to his secretary, telling her to send Peters in his place to the Viceroy meeting at the Savoy.

'But he's already scheduled to see someone,' Rosemary protested uselessly.

'Then he'll just have to cancel, won't he?'

'But...'

'I'm leaving the office. I can't go. That's all there is to it. In case it's missed you, Rosemary, I pay these people to handle important meetings. They'll just have to start earning their keep.'

'Of course, but...' She sighed. 'Are you feeling all right, Mr Ross?'

'Of course *I'm feeling all right*. Is there any reason why I shouldn't be? Do I sound ill to you?'

'Not *ill*, no...' Rosemary's voice trailed significantly down the end of the line and he had to stop himself from clicking his tongue in annoyance. He'd seen enough looks and been privy to sufficient concerned remarks to know what was coming next and he wasn't in the mood for it.

'It's just that you never take time off work, and you have three meetings this afternoon...'

'A simple request, Rosemary, that's all it was. A simple request to cancel my appointments for today so that I can leave the office. I fail to see what the problem is.'

'You haven't been yourself recently, Mr Ross,' Rosemary said in a burst of courage. 'Several of us have been...'

'*Several of you?* I pay you people to work, not to gather into little covens discussing my welfare.'

'How long do you intend to be out of the office, Mr Ross?' she said, returning to her normal brisk voice, and Callum sucked in his breath, realising that an apology was called for but temporarily incapable of dispensing one. Anyone would think that his employees had nothing better to do than shadow his every movement and watch his every expression.

'I have no idea. One day, two days—maybe longer.'

'So what shall I do about...?'

'Rearrange everything in the foreseeable future. When I come back, you can schedule my time.' On which note, he disconnected the internal line and remained sitting for a few minutes longer, staring into space and brooding.

It was becoming an addiction.

Memory lane was now so well trodden that it was beginning to seem more real than what was happening in his life at the moment.

He fished into his trouser pocket, took out his wallet and extracted a crumpled piece of paper from one of the compartments.

It was a fairly pointless procedure, since he knew what was written on the paper by heart, but still he hung on to it, compulsively reading and re-reading the handful of lines that had been waiting for him two months ago on his return from New York.

She had, regrettably, turned down his proposal, she'd written, though she'd appreciated the offer. Under the circumstances, she felt that nothing further would be gained by remaining in England, and was thereby handing over responsibility for the sale of the company to Derek.

He savagely scanned the note, his mouth tightening, as it always did, when he came to the bit about wishing him all the best for the future.

Enraged, as if reading it for the first time, he crumpled the paper, then reluctantly smoothed it out and replaced it in the wallet. Then he strode to the door, flinging on his jacket in the process, and out into the connecting room where Rosemary glanced up from her computer with long-suffering wariness.

'Look,' he said awkwardly, 'I'm sorry if I overreacted just then.'

'That's all right,' Rosemary said quietly.

'I've had a lot on my mind recently...'

'Of course. I understand. Felt Pharmaceuticals has taken a lot of financial resources out of the company profits. Naturally, that would be on your mind...'

'Naturally,' Callum said, going along with that piece of fiction. In truth, the temporary drain on his financial well-being had barely crossed his mind. Within a year things would have evened out, and within a couple of years Felt's would be more than paying for itself. Life would have been a piece of cake if his only worries centred around something as piddling and unimportant as money.

'It would help if you could call me when you're about

to come back,' she said, absently flicking through the diary, which, standing above her, he could see was liberally speckled with entries. Important meetings with important people to discuss important things. Who cared?

'I'll try,' he said slowly. 'But I'm not sure how feasible that will be.' For the first time in a little over two months he managed something resembling a smile, and Rosemary offered a tentative one back in return. 'Where I'm going, the phone lines might be a little bit erratic.' He felt a wild thrill soar through him as his decision was made. No more mindless, brooding introspection, spending every waking moment haunted by images of her while he outwardly attempted to control the reins of his life and convince himself that he was better off without her around. He would go, he would find her and, if nothing else, he would get her to explain how someone could strain in his arms and then hours later bid him farewell via a note and without a backward glance.

She'd gone and he hadn't even told her that he loved her. Pride and fear of being rejected had held him back, and he was willing to shed both even if it meant trekking back to England with nothing but his wounds to nurse in private.

He packed a suitcase like a man demented, remembering her descriptions of the stifling heat and her gentle amusement at Derek's garb when he'd shown up on their compound. He flung in tee-shirts and the only three pairs of shorts he could rustle up, and underwear, and then an assorted selection of other items which he hoped would tide him over.

Then he telephoned the airport and, after an aggressive approach, during which he didn't hesitate to mention every influential name he remotely knew working in the airline industry, managed to secure a seat on the next plane out to Panama the following day.

Destiny eyed her class with a jaundiced and resigned expression. Today, only five children had shown up. The rains had come and the missing faces had caved in at the prospect of a walk in sodden undergrowth in pelting rainfall. Three were ill with the fever, which meant that she would probably have to do the trip with her father later in the evening to make sure that the fever was confinable and not something more rampant and sinister. It was a prospect that made her heart sink.

Ever since returning to Panama she'd found that the simple enthusiasm with which she'd greeted these physical and tiring duties had been difficult to muster. And there was no one in whom she could confide. Henri had taken extended leave and was currently in Paris at his mother's bedside, tending her through the final stages of a cancer about which he'd known nothing until he'd got to England, and to confess to her father that she missed England would break his heart. He needed her and she had to respond to that need, even though her heart was no longer in it. At least, not in the way it used to be. She still efficiently did what she had to do, but in the manner of an automaton, completing functions so that it could then shut down, leaving her private time to think back. Her desperate dash back to Panama, far from assuaging her wounded heart, had been a failure. The torment she'd sought to escape had dogged her right back to the jungle and showed no signs of letting up.

And the weather wasn't helping matters. The rains this time round were considerable, and she felt as though she was literally and figuratively drowning.

'You'd better go home for the day,' she said at a little

after twelve, when the rain was threatening to turn into a storm. She could barely make herself heard above the crashing of the rain against the window panes. 'And, Paolo, make sure that your brothers do some reading.' She managed a weak smile, ushering her little troop to the door and making them don plastic hoods which were fairly useless in a downpour of this nature and anyway would probably be merrily discarded the minute the compound was out of sight.

It was surreal to think that less than three months ago she had been in England, wearing clothes that looked like clothes and shoes that were ornamental rather than useful. She glanced across the open courtyard and through the driving rain saw her father beckoning to her.

'An emergency!' he was yelling, although the noise swept away a good part of what he was saying, and Destiny sighed and nodded, hurrying along the corridors of the wooden building and emerging a few minutes later through the door to her father's office.

'Apologise for disrupting your class, darling.' He ran his fingers through his sparse, greying hair and gave her a worried look. 'I've been radioed from El Real that there's an emergency.'

'What kind of emergency?'

'Lone tourist has bumped into some of our mosquitoes and contracted some kind of parasitic infection. Or, at least, that's what Enrique seems to think, but he's no doctor.'

'What about the medical services there?' Though 'medical services' was something of an overstatement to describe the sole hard-working doctor with whom they had fairly regular communication.

'Pablo's been called away for another emergency a few kilometres away and seems to have become stranded out there by the rains. Dessie, I know you probably don't want to do this, but there's no one else. If Henri had been here I would have asked him, but, really, with me gone I'd need our own qualified doctor here just in case. We've had to deal with two snake bites already in the past couple of days, and Lord knows what's happening towards Cana. I've had reports of fevers.' He looked as weary as she had ever seen him.

'Right. I'll get something packed.' She carried on discussing their method of transport, none too reliable in the current deluge, but she could feel her heart sinking fast. Her father was right. She didn't want to go. There was enough to do here and the trip, which would probably take hours and be a nightmare journey, filled her with sudden dismay.

All she wanted to do was huddle away in her room and let her mind travel back through time.

Within the hour they had told the various other members of the compound what was happening, and were climbing into their four-wheel drive.

The journey would be a combination of road and river and promised to be hellish. Despite the onslaught of rain the atmosphere was stifling and humid, and she knew that, given the muddy nature of the pathways linking all these small towns, they would spend at least a proportion of their time clearing morass from the roads in an attempt to get through. It was always the same during the rainy seasons, and this time it would be a thousand times worse because of the quantity of rainfall.

'It's ridiculous,' Destiny told her father, as they progressed at a snail's pace, with the wipers going at a rate. 'Why do tourists feel that they can travel unaided into this part of the world? What gives them the right to expect help when they get themselves into a muddle?'

'This sounds a little worse than a lost tourist who's got into a muddle,' her father said, craning forward to make sure that he kept to the barely visible marked path.

'We'll get there and he'll have nothing more than a few mosquito bites and a bad cold from getting soaked.'

'Not from what Enrique says.'

'Enrique runs the grocery store and a rooming house!' Destiny grumbled on insistently. 'He's not likely to be much of a gem when it comes to diagnosing illnesses! Did he say what the symptoms were?'

'Raging fever, apparently. The man's hallucinating.'

'I feel like I'm about to hallucinate,' she said, wiping her face with the rag she had brought with her. 'This car is going to self-combust in a minute.' The windows were rolled down, but only very slightly to allow for the rain and the heat inside the car was fierce. Even with the miniature fan affixed to the dashboard she could still feel beads of sweat rolling down her face and making her body feel like oil. She rolled her glass down a few more centimetres and was rewarded with a wash of water across her face. It was better, at any rate, than the humidity.

'I never really asked you this, Destiny, but what exactly happened out there in England?' Her father wasn't looking at her, and she felt a little jolt of shock at his question. He was a reticent man when it came to conversations about feelings and emotions, and for him to encourage one right now showed how much the question had been nagging away at the back of his mind.

'Nothing happened out there.'

'The last time we spoke when you were there, you seemed to have settled in and you were enjoying yourself.'

'I never said that I was *enjoying* myself,' she persisted

stubbornly, staring out of the window as the rain lashed the rainforest around them, making every bending tree and swirling leaf look dangerous. Men thought that they were so big and strong. Well, it only took one show of nature like this to silence them.

'Darling, you don't actually *need* to spell everything out for me. I know I'm an old duffer—'

'Dad! Don't!'

'—but I can occasionally read between the lines, and you were enjoying yourself. Nothing like that time when you were in Mexico and you were so desperate to come back home.'

They both paused as the car was manoeuvred very slowly through a minor flood, densely brown and littered with fallen leaves.

'So why did you suddenly decide to leave?'

'I didn't suddenly decide,' Destiny said awkwardly. 'I just realised that I couldn't accomplish any more over there, so I came back.'

'Henri said something about a man.'

'Henri? What did he say? It's not true!'

'He said something about this Callum character...'

'Henri doesn't know Callum from Adam!' she burst out, cursing her friend for having dumped her in the mire. She hadn't mentioned Callum Ross to her father because there had been no point. It would only have hurt and disappointed him to think that she'd got caught up in a temporary and seedy affair with someone so alien to the sort of man he would have expected for her. Not a doctor, not someone whose life-blood was rooted in environmental issues and helping other people. But a business-man. Someone whose interests were all wrapped up in making money, even when it involved marrying a woman to further his ends.

'What was he like, then?'

'What was who like?'

'You're dodging the question. And you're going into a sulk.'

'Dad, I'm a grown woman. Grown women don't go into sulks. Have you ever known me to go into a sulk?'

'No,' he admitted, but before she could give a triumphant smile, he carried on remorselessly, 'which is why your behaviour has been so odd ever since you returned. You say the right things, and never hesitate to pull your weight, but you've been wrapped up in yourself and I can't help but wonder whether something happened to you over there that you're not telling me about. If I didn't know better, I'd say that you're suffering all the symptoms of love sickness.'

'Oh, Dad, *please.*' Amazing how parents had a knack of making you feel like a child.

'And the only name that's been mentioned in connection with your stay in England, aside from the Wilson man, is this Callum character.'

'Who is just the sort of man I would never fall in love with!' She thought back to that hard, intelligent face, those skilful hands that had explored every inch of her body until she'd thought she would suffocate from desire—and then she thought of his proposal, which had been like a punch in her gut. Cold, logical, without feeling or emotion. Theoretically, the sort of man she really would never fall in love with, which just went to show how huge the gap was between theory and practice.

'Why?' her father was asking in a mildly curious voice. 'Is he cruel? A bore? Stupid?'

'No, none of those things.'

'Ah. I see,' her father murmured.

'He just expects everything to go his way, even when

his plans are…are…' Her cheeks were bright red, and not from the sweltering heat in the car. She stopped abruptly, caught off guard in the middle of her sentence. 'He thinks that because things make some kind of peculiar sense to him everyone will just fall into line and go along with what he has to offer.'

'Are we talking about his purchase of the company? Because, from the sounds of it, it seemed very generous, and it's a great relief to me that you now have more than sufficient funds to retire to England whenever you choose…'

Destiny looked at her father as though he had suddenly taken leave of his senses. What was he talking about? Ever since she had returned to Panama she'd felt as though, subtly but undeniably, things were changing around her. No comfortable Henri, no comfortable routines that she never questioned, and now her father was hinting that she might want to go back to England. Why?

'I don't intend to go back there,' Destiny said quickly. 'Why should I?'

'Why indeed?' her father said, which wasn't much of an answer. 'We should be hitting the station in the next hour or so, if the weather conditions don't get any worse; then we can get a boat to Real. With any luck, the river's going to be all right.'

'If the boatmen haven't all holed up for the rains,' Destiny said gloomily.

By the time they finally made it to the station, the dubious quality of the light was beginning to fade and, as she had feared, they were compelled to spend the night at the ranger station. There was no electricity, and bathing in the creek was out of the question because of the weather, so, after a basic meal, which was brought by them but cooked in good humour by Juan, who refused to see the massive rains as anything other than a minor nuisance, Destiny retired to her cot, sticky, muddy and dishevelled. Her feet felt stiff from the hiking boots she had worn. All around here was fer de lance territory and the thought of a snake bite further complicating things was not even to be contemplated. No one ventured out without the protection of boots. Useful, necessary, but unfortunately very conducive to sweaty feet.

Juan, because he knew them and liked them, had managed to provide two pails of creek water, so at least she found she could go to sleep with clean feet, if very little else.

And the rains, overnight, appeared to have let up a bit. She awakened to more of a persistent drizzle than the torrential, never-ending downpour that had been in evidence over the past few weeks.

'I hope your cousin's going to do the boat trip for us,' Destiny said to Juan once they were outside, 'and he hasn't got himself into one of his alcoholic jags.'

'José's given up the evil drink.' Juan grinned, while Destiny shot him a long, sceptical look. 'No, really!' he said, holding his hands up. 'I think it was after that lecture you gave him.'

'Well, your mother will be pleased.'

'Now all he has to do is find a wife and give her some grandchildren.'

'At seventeen?'

'Never too young to start.' He eyed her cheekily. 'I'd advise you not to leave it too long, old lady.' To which she told him to shut up, but she was in a less oppressed frame of mind by the time they began the second leg of their journey, boxes of provisions and clothes in hand, as well as invaluable medical supplies which were contained in a watertight box and wrapped in several layers of waterproof plastic for good measure.

As soon as they arrived at Enrique's house, her father turned to her and told her to stay put.

'I'll make a diagnosis and then we can discuss what we need to do.'

He vanished inside the room while Destiny remained outside, staring at the fine grey drizzle and trying to come to terms with a life that had been stood on its head and even now was moving at newer and crazier angles with each passing moment. She jumped when her father finally reappeared.

'It's serious, Dessie. Dengue fever. His fever's through the roof and apparently he's been slipping in and out of consciousness. I've washed him a bit, and changed him, but we need to start administering antibiotics in case secondary infections have set in. So...'

She nodded. She knew the routine. She also knew that round-the-clock antibiotics would require them both to take turns at getting up in the early hours of the morning to inject him. Under normal circumstances, and if they'd been in the makeshift hospital area in the compound, they would have had the facilities to give the antibiotics via a drip, but it would be more rudimentary here.

'Will he pull through?' she asked, following her father to the room, and he shrugged and gave a fifty-fifty gesture with his hand.

'Take a look for yourself and then tell me what you think. I haven't seen a case of Dengue this bad for a while...'

Destiny approached the bed, sympathetic to the tourist's plight but exasperated by his foolishness in thinking he could undertake a trek of mammoth proportions in damaging weather.

What she saw made the colour drain away from her face. She felt her breathing thicken. Her father was talking behind her, but his voice was background noise, insignificant next to the roaring in her head.

Callum Ross, ashen and unshaven, lay on the bed. And he was dying. She could almost see the life ebbing away from him as she continued to stare, until the ground began to feel unsteady under her feet and she reached out to support herself on the side of the bed.

'We'll do our best,' her father said quietly, approaching her, 'but it's a bad case.'

'It's Callum Ross,' she whispered, turning stricken eyes to her father. 'The man is Callum Ross.'

'What the...?'

'Please, Dad. Let me give him the antibiotics.' But her hand was shaking so much that she couldn't, and her father swiftly injected him.

She remained with him for the rest of the day, watching the flicker of eyelids over closed eyes, checking him frequently to see whether the tell tale rash that marked the end of the fever was beginning to appear.

'You fool,' she whispered, reaching out to hold his hand. 'What got into your head? Don't die on me, Callum. I'll never forgive you.' One tear spilled down her face and was quickly joined by another. When, later, her father came in to administer the next lot of medicine, she was steady enough to do it herself, and she hustled him out of the door, nodding feverishly when he told her what needed doing.

His body, which had filled every corner of her mind for the past couple of months, seemed vulnerable now that it was under attack. When she washed him, she could see the signs of wasting already beginning to set in. He wouldn't have eaten for days, and the stubble on his face was beginning to resemble the start of a beard.

'I could shave you,' she said, speaking to herself, because thus far she had had no response from him. 'Would you trust me to do that? Why couldn't you have stayed put?' she demanded, swerving away from the subject and glaring at him. 'If you've put yourself in danger because of a couple of questions you wanted to ask about the business, then I'll kill you, Callum Ross. Do you hear me?' No, of course he didn't, but she carried on talking anyway, all through the night, until sleep finally overcame her.

She was awake at the crack of dawn, leaving him alone only long enough to freshen herself and grab something to eat. She was barely aware of her father's battery of questions and offered no explanations.

When she returned to the room, it was to find that Callum at least had changed position on the bed. He was no longer on his back, with his grey face upturned, but on his side, even though his eyes were still closed.

And his breathing seemed easier as well, although she was well aware that that was probably her imagination. It was easy to become accustomed to the varying patterns of an illness until you imagined that they were less severe than they had been at the outset.

She propped him gently up and tried to spoon some liquid food down him.

'Have I told you that you're a fool, Callum Ross?' she said, growing accustomed to the sensation of making conversation into silence to someone who couldn't hear what she was saying. 'Didn't I tell you about the mishaps that happened to tourists who took risks?'

She heard the tremor in her voice. 'Dad's asking a million questions about you and I don't know what to tell him. He wants to know why I'm insisting on doing everything for you when I've explained to him what an arrogant, irritating thorn under the skin you are. He wants to know why I'm running around like a headless chicken and looking like a washed-out rag over someone I told him doesn't matter. He can't understand what you're doing in this part of the world. As usual, I'm in a mess because of you.'

She expertly took his temperature and logged it on the frightening chart that was now clipped to the top of the bed, then she sat back and looked at the man lying on the bed in front of her. 'You risked your life...for what? Some papers I may have forgotten to sign? You stupid man.' Her voice was beginning to sound unnatural again, and she breathed in deeply in an attempt to control it.

She was slowly realising that, even though she'd come back to Panama, even though she'd told herself that Panama was her country and she would remain there for evermore, doing what she'd always done, even if she died a sad, old spinster, a part of her had still believed that one day she would see him again. Because miracles happened. If Callum died now, then there would be no miracles.

Over the next day, she continued with her routine, mopping him, feeding him in a ritual that could take anything up to an hour, watching and waiting and waiting and watching, barely sleeping herself.

All she wanted was one word from him, a signal that he was on the mend.

'He's not going downhill, at any rate,' her father said on the third day, as he stood next to her and performed a number of routine examinations. 'In fact, the fever's beginning to let up a bit.' Instead of leaving the room this time, he walked slowly across to the window and stood there with his back to it.

'And I want some answers from you, young woman.'

'What answers? I can't predict the outcome of this any more than you can, Dad,' Destiny said, deliberately misreading his question, even though she knew that it was no more than a temporary stalling exercise.

'What's the relationship between you and this young man?'

'Relationship? *Relationship?*'

'That's right.' He had an implacable glint in his eye which she met with a mutinous look.

'I'm just looking after him the way I'd look after any idiot who managed to get themselves in this situation because they were too bull-headed to admit that they couldn't cope with the rigours of a journey way beyond their experience.'

Her father didn't say anything. He just continued to look at her patiently, while Callum lay inert on the bed between them.

'Okay!' she half-shouted, glaring at her father and that infernally mild expression of his which had always been more effective when it came to getting what he wanted than any Chinese water torture method. 'So we may have seen one another now and again when I was in England! Is it my fault that the man's pushy?' She folded her arms and watched as her father slowly moved towards the bed so that they were now facing each other with only the width of the bed between them. 'One minute there he was, using every trick in the book to get the company off me, and the next minute…the next minute he's forcing himself on me so that I have no option but to have dinner with him!'

'Ah.'

'Okay! So I may have...may have found him attractive...' She gave her father a weak, apologetic smile. 'Not,' she said, addressing the man on the bed because her situation was all thanks to him, 'that you look very attractive at the moment, Callum Ross! But then whose idiot fault is that?' Panic and worry made her want to strangle him and hold him tightly at the same time.

'So my little girl went to England and grew up,' her father mused slowly to himself.

'If by *growing up,* you call falling in love with the least suitable man on the face of the earth!' She tenderly stroked his forehead.

'I suspected as much.'

'It's not going to come to anything!' Destiny cried. 'He doesn't love me!'

'But you love him.'

'Life's just not fair, is it, Dad? You and Mum just clicked, but me...I had to go halfway across the world and get myself embroiled with a hardheaded businessman who doesn't know the meaning of love.'

'How do you know that?'

She sighed in resignation. 'Because he proposed to me, but *not,*' she carried on quickly, seeing the interruption forming on her father's lips, 'because he loved me. He said that an alliance would make a good business proposition. He wanted my company, we got along, and to him it made sense that we should just tie the two things together and bingo, a marriage made in heaven.' Now she was beginning to feel like a sixteen-year-old child again. Moreover, she didn't want the compassion she could see in her father's eyes. A little bit of shared hostility might have got her going on the right path, but compassion was just going to make her break down.

'So there you go. That's the relationship. I love him,

and now you know I want you to promise not to mention it again.'

They stared at one another, and then, from the bed, Callum said, 'But I was getting really interested in all of this. Please, carry on. Don't mind me.'

CHAPTER TEN

'ARE you sure it's all right for you to be here? Anything could happen.'

'Don't be such a wimp.' Destiny stepped out into the dense, inky blackness and reached out for the hand waiting for her, which slipped around her waist, pulling her against him.

'Wimp? Me? That's not what your father thinks.' Callum buried his face against her hair and reached to cup the side of her head with his hand. 'In fact,' he murmured in a satisfied voice, tickling her ear with his breath, 'if I recall, he told you how lucky you were to meet me.'

'He may have been delusional.' She was grinning as the hot night air wafted aromatically around them. In the compound, everyone was asleep, unlike outside, where the animals of the night had come out to play and could be heard calling from the trees and beyond into the depths of the forest.

They walked slowly and entwined, to one of the three benches which had been recently placed in a circular format under a spreading tree, making it a wonderful place for some of the women to do their craft-making during the day, protected from the full-frontal attack of the sun.

Nine months had changed a lot, not least on the compound, where sensibly-spent money had improved living conditions and amassed more much-needed staff to cope with Henri's departure, her own and, in due course, her father's. He would be working in the medical facilities of the Felt Pharmaceutical subsidiary, which had now only been going for a matter of a few weeks.

Nine months of absolute bliss. It still seemed hard to believe that dreams had come true...

When Callum, supposedly on his death bed and utterly unconscious to anything happening around him, had murmured those words, Destiny had been overcome by the twin emotions of shock and mortification.

They had both stared down at the bed to find Callum looking at them, eyes open and with an expression which, if not perky, had been amused enough to inform her that his brush with death had been successfully outmanoeuvred.

'My boy, you're with us at last.' Her father scurried around, taking all the routine medical checks, making sure that everything was now returning to the land of the living.

All Destiny could think of to say was, 'How long have you been listening to our conversation?'

'Is that any way to greet the man you adore, when he's been on the brink of death?'

Aside from his voice sounding weaker, any near-death experience had certainly left his mind as alert as ever it had been and his sense of humour utterly intact.

'Which,' she hissed, bending down to look at him, at once gutted by such an enormous feeling of relief that he was out of the woods that it was quite possible to allow her embarrassed anger at being eavesdropped to get the better of her, 'he has clearly managed to overcome.' He'd put her through hell, and now here he was, frail, haggard, feeble—yet still capable of rousing within her emotions that left no room for anything else.

What a consummate actor! Lying there on the bed. Had

he heard everything she had told her father? Every word?
And had he been aware all along of her presence in the
room, hovering over him like a desperate mother hen, not
bothering to hide her tears at night because she'd fool-
ishly imagined that he couldn't hear them?

What did it matter, anyway? He had heard enough.

'Don't pester the man, Dessie,' her father ordered, un-
able to hear their *sotto voce* conversation but more than
capable of hearing the tenor of her voice, which contained no hint of any soothing bedside manner.

'Yes, my worshipping nurse, a little sympathy, please.'
Callum gave her a weak, pathetic smile, and then added
insult to injury by asking her whether she would mind
feeding him a little something, because he really was
quite hungry now.

'Does he think this is a hotel?' Destiny fulminated to
her father, once they were safely out of the choking confines of the room, which seemed to have shrunk to the
size of a matchbox the minute Callum opened his eyes.
And his mouth, for that matter.

'He may be conscious, but he obviously hasn't had a
good look around at his surroundings as yet,' she chun-
tered on, ignoring her father's lack of input into the conversation. 'He might just have realised that rustling up a
few tasty morsels might be a tad more difficult than he
thinks!'

'We could see our way to bread and soup, Dessie,' her
father reminded her gently. 'There's no need to take it
out on the poor man just because he happened to over-
hear what you were saying to me about—'

'Don't remind me!' Destiny nearly wailed, slopping
soup into a bowl, then carefully re-covering it to protect
it from the flies.

'He's been through a bad experience. Can you imagine

how hideous this whole thing must have been for him? The man nearly died, for goodness's sake!'

'I'm not saying that I'm not glad he's on the mend. I'm just saying that the two-faced cad had a right to let us know what was going on before I embarked on my soul-wrenching confession. But oh, no! *Typical!*'

She then proceeded to spend the next two days running and fetching for him. In her father's presence he professed to be much weaker than he was, refusing to answer any of her questions with a feeble wave of his hand whilst still being able to insist that she sit with him while he fed himself, taking ages in the process, and that she talk to him because, although he couldn't possibly communicate for any length of time, he still needed to feel the presence of other people around him. By 'other people,' he meant her. And having her around gave him ample opportunity to remind her of the heart-wrenching confession he had wilfully overheard.

He constantly asked her if she really was her beloved darling, and when she refused to answer smiled in an infuriatingly knowing way.

By the end of day two her father assured her that Callum was fit enough to travel back to the compound. The rains had almost completely stopped, he could now walk unaided—even though he still made a great production of it and insisted on clutching her arm whenever she was around—and her father needed to return to his base.

The trip was accomplished in half the time and without the sweltering discomfort of the drive to the outpost, and by the time they arrived back at the compound Destiny was determined to pin him to a wall until he told her why he'd made the trip in the first place.

If he had come for a signature on something, then she

would give it to him and send him on his way, because being so close to him with her feelings so nakedly exposed was tearing her apart. The constant feel of his body against hers as he used her as a propping post sent ragged emotions flying through her, and the whole business was driving her crazy.

She had fled to Panama to escape him, and now found herself in the worst possible spot she could have imagined. He'd discovered how she felt about him and he was determined to wrench every ounce of advantage that he could from the situation.

No opportunity to remind her of her regrettable confession was left unturned. When he wasn't insisting on her personal attention she felt him watching her, but stoically refused to meet his eyes and see the smug knowledge resting there.

If this was his way of getting his own back on her for having run out on him and his cold-hearted marriage proposal, then he had hit jackpot.

As soon as she'd ensconced him in the room he would be having until he was ready to leave, she closed the door behind them and stood there, hands on hips, watching as he indolently took the chair by the window.

'You can stop pretending now,' she informed him without preamble, ignoring the innocently raised eyebrows forming a question. 'And you can stop playing the innocent. You know exactly what I'm talking about.'

'Should you really be taking this tone with someone who's still recovering from a near-death experience?'

'If you don't cut it out, Callum Ross, you'll be facing another near-death experience and it won't be caused by a mosquito! Don't think that I'm too stupid to see through your little games.'

'What little games?' More innocent enquiry in his

voice until she wanted to scream. Instead, she swallowed hard and took a couple of deep, reviving breaths.

'So I ran out on you. Maybe I should have stayed in England and told you to your face that I wasn't about to enter into marriage with someone who saw me as a useful commodity with the added bonus of sex toy until the novelty wore off. I was a coward, but...'

'And now I understand why,' he murmured, in such a soft voice that she had to reluctantly install herself closer to where he was just to hear him properly.

'Yes,' Destiny said bitterly, 'now you know why. And you're basking in the knowledge, aren't you? Your ego must have taken a bashing when you got back from New York to find that I'd disappeared, but you've had your little gloat now. If you came here for me to sign something, then give it to me, let me sign it, and then you can go and leave me alone to get on with my life.' A red mist of self-pity and lurking humiliation formed over her eyes like a cloud.

'And what if I came here to propose to you again?' he asked softly.

'Then you can go back to England and remember what I wrote in that note. The answer is still no.'

'You love me...'

The words were like a dagger jutting into her soft flesh. 'It'll pass,' she told him acidly. 'Like an illness. But there's no way that you'll use what you know to your advantage. Anyway, what would be the point of marrying me now? You got what you wanted all along. I kept the properties and you got the company.'

'Maybe I want the country house as well,' he murmured, looking at her unflinchingly.

'To develop? Something else to add to your portfolio?'

'Maybe I want to live there... It would be a rather

spectacular place for a family...lots of space for lots of kids...'

The words swam seductively around her.

'Then you'd better start looking for a woman you love,' she said in a dull monotone, alarmed by the flight of fancy that had taken her back to the country estate, but this time with this man by her side and children romping around by their feet. A charming little tableau, she thought, were it not for one or two glaring technicalities.

'Why would I do that?' he asked, tilting his head to one side quizzically. 'When I've already found her?'

'Stop it,' she whispered. Tears were gathering in the corners of her eyes and she angrily blinked them away, coincidentally blinking away the vision of him in front of her, looking at her in that way, that way that suggested the impossible, even though she knew that he was still playing games with her.

'No, I won't. I can't,' he said huskily, so that now a desperate kind of hope was beginning to wage war with her grim acceptance. And, like a weed, the hope was sending out shoots everywhere.

'What are you talking about?' Destiny asked in a small, despairing voice.

'I'm talking about you and me and why I trudged half-way across the world to get here. All for you. I don't need your signature on anything aside from on a marriage licence.'

'I told you...'

'You're not listening, my darling.'

It was the tenderness in his voice that did it. She looked at him fully in the face, willing him to say what she wanted to hear but bracing herself in case the words she craved veered off somewhere along the line, just as they had done the last time. She reminded herself viciously that this was but one moment in time, and if it proved a bad moment then it would be washed away eventually and become no more painful than a distant memory. He would go; she would stay; life would carry on the way it always did. Hadn't it been carrying along for the past two months, ever since she had returned from England? She hadn't died from a broken heart, had she?

'I came here to tell you that...' His words dried up and a faint flush began spreading along his neck. 'That...when you ran out on me like that...' He raked long fingers through his hair and told her that he could do with some water, which she refused to get.

'I'm still very weak.'

'Carry on with what you were saying.'

'When you ran out on me like that...' he continued, like a record that had become stuck in a groove.

'Yes?' She had every intention of pushing the needle a bit further.

'I...it was like a punch in the stomach...'

'Oh.'

He tilted her face to his and ran his finger along the side of her cheek. 'No, I'm lying. It was much, much worse than that. It was like watching my life run away down a gutter because...I love you. That's why I came here. To tell you that I love you.'

'To tell me that you love me.' The phrase tasted so delightfully delicious on her lips, did such soaring things to her heart, that she just wanted to repeat it over and over again. She laughed incredulously. 'Because *you* love *me*. Because,' she said, relishing the revelation, 'you love *me*.'

'And because, my darling, I want to marry you. I want to have you by my side and in my bed for the rest of my

life. Because I want you to have my babies and be there
with them, waiting for me at the end of a long day. To
touch, to hold, to caress, to grow old with me, to laugh
with me, to do everything under the sun with me.'

'Penny for them.'
The deep voice interrupted her thoughts and she smiled
to herself in the dark. 'I was thinking about…everything.'
She rested her head against his shoulder. 'About us, the
wedding, and now this…'
She patted her stomach and felt a warm glow of contentment.
'We'll have to bring him back here, you know. Or her.
To see where I lived for so long. He won't be able to
believe it when he's running around the grounds of the
house, that his mother ran around different grounds when
she was young. And with Dad leaving I feel a little as if
part of me is vanishing for ever.'
'It's not vanishing,' Callum said softly. 'It's something
that's shaped you and will be with you for ever. It's just
given way to something else, a different way of life. And
of course we'll be back to Panama often, to see your
father when he's here.'
'You mean, your fan?' she teased. Far from disliking
Callum, her father had warmed to him instantly, and the
pride on his face at their small wedding still had the
power to make her feel tearful.
'One of my fans,' he said airily. 'The other one's here
next to me and number three will be on the scene in a
matter of three months. What more could any man ask
for?'
Or woman, for that matter, she thought lazily. Who
could ask for any more perfection?

EPILOGUE

'WELL, I think it's time we decided to go for it. There'll be one or two changes to your lifestyle... Could you cope...? Do you even *want* to cope? Am I presuming too much?'

'How can you even think that you're presuming too much? After all the things I've told you, you little fool. I can't imagine any kind of life without you in it...'

'So if I asked you to marry me, your answer would be...?'

'Yes! Yes, a thousand times over! Yes, yes, yes!'

There was much fumbling, then a small box was retrieved from a trouser pocket. The look in her eyes, eyes that could still turn his bones to water, made the unaccustomed and arduous hike through jewellery shops worth every minute of exhaustion.

'My mother is going to be so pleased,' he murmured with blushing pleasure.

'*Only* your mother?'

'Pleased doesn't begin to tell you what I feel now. I'm walking on cloud nine. But...'

'No buts.' She slipped the ring onto her finger and held it up to the light, letting herself be dazzled by the solitaire glow from the diamond.

'Panama is completely different from London,' he said gravely.

'One city is much the same as another when you're with someone you love,' she answered in as grave a voice as his. And she meant every word of it. She closed her

186

eyes and sighed with happiness as he leaned across the small table in the restaurant to place a kiss on her mouth, a kiss that was as tender as it was laden with the heady promise of the life stretching out before them.

Everything was so different and so good. She was even beginning to learn French, to be as bilingual as he was.

'And,' he said, sitting back and leaning with his elbows resting on the table, 'how do you feel about starting a family? I have to admit that when we went to see Destiny and Callum and their baby, I felt a little envious.'

'I know. Little Rosie's perfect, isn't she? Those green, green eyes and black, black hair.' She smiled at the memory of her one-time fiancé and his fierce devotion to the two women in his life. Destiny and baby Rose. He had barely been able to tear his proud eyes away from the two of them.

'Yes, my darling Henri,' Stephanie said dreamily, 'I think starting a family would be a very good idea indeed...'

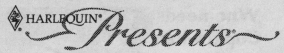

WITH HARLEQUIN AND SILHOUETTE

There's a romance to fit your every mood.

Passion

Harlequin Temptation

Harlequin Presents

Silhouette Desire

Pure Romance

Harlequin Romance

Silhouette Romance

Home & Family

Harlequin
American Romance

Silhouette
Special Edition

A Longer Story
With More

Harlequin
Superromance

Suspense & Adventure

Harlequin Intrigue

Silhouette Intimate
Moments

Humor

Harlequin Duets

Historical

Harlequin Historicals

Special Releases

Other great
romances
to explore

HARLEQUIN *Presents*

The world's bestselling romance series... The series that brings you your favorite authors, month after month:

Helen Bianchin
Emma Darcy
Lynne Graham
Penny Jordan
Miranda Lee
Sandra Marton
Anne Mather
Carole Mortimer
Susan Napier
Michelle Reid

and many more uniquely talented authors!

Wealthy, powerful, gorgeous men...Women who have feelings just like your own... The stories you love, set in glamorous, international locations

HARLEQUIN PRESENTS®
Seduction and passion guaranteed!

Available wherever Harlequin books are sold.